OPERATION: CRIMSON DECEIT

Written By Zane Raub

Dedication

For my late mother, Shirley, whose curiosity for history inspired my own. This is a tribute to her enduring legacy.

Table of Contents

Acknowledgements

While I should have been focused on work, my mind was wandering after a conversation I had with a coworker. He had previously lived in Kazakhstan and shared a story or two about life in Russia, both from a personal and historical perspective. From that conversation with my friend Nerlan, an idea was born—an idea of something that might have happened or could have happened. Either way, it got me thinking about how it could unfold. And so, the story began: the inspiration to write about a "what if" scenario. I find it impossible not to thank my dear and kind friend Nerlan for sparking that idea.

To Dawn: You were the first person I shared my story with. Throughout the years, you kept encouraging me to write this story. You never wavered. You offered ideas and support, and for that, I thank you.

To my brother Scott: You also inherited our mother's fascination with history. Thank you not only for everything you do but also for being the perfect big brother.

To my friends and colleagues: Rich, Dave, Wayne, Gary, Patty, Shayne, Joe, the Wendt family, the Deering family, my Tecmotiv family and my Shawnee Indians family—thank you for your kindness and friendship.

To the rest of my family: Dad, Lori, the Bandura family, Sonie, and Justine—thank you for your love and support.

A huge thank you to the team at Amazon Publishing for making this possible.

To my daughters, Heather and Alyssa, and my honey, Marie: Thank you for giving me a reason to make this happen.

Lastly, to my readers, who chose this story in the hopes of finding an escape, to daydream, and maybe even wonder, like I do, about how things were and to ask the question of "what if." Thank you for taking this journey with me.

With gratitude,

Zane Raub

Chapter 1:
Recall

Elana's breath formed frosty plumes as she trudged through the freshly fallen snow. The winter sun, a pale smear in the overcast sky, barely touched the icy sidewalks of Buffalo, New York. The streets were bustling with the early Christmas rush, shop windows dressed in festive garlands and twinkling lights, a nod to the post-war prosperity that had swept across America.

As Elana passed by the grand art deco facade of the North Park Theatre, now showing "Vertigo," a recent Hitchcock thriller, the marquee lights flickered against the gray sky, casting a warm glow on the snow below. Clutching her grocery bags tightly against her side, Elana wrapped her thick, woolen scarf closer around her neck, shielding her face from the biting wind that swept down the street. Despite the harsh cold that would have deterred most, her weathered face showed a seasoned resilience—she was no stranger to the fierce winters here, having braved them since childhood.

As she approached the modest two-story house that had been her home for decades, Elana's pace quickened with the thought of the warmth awaiting her inside. She shuffled up the porch steps, dusting off snow that clung to her coat. Before entering, she paused at the mailbox, her fingers numb as she fumbled through the assortment of bills and holiday cards. Among them, a striking red envelope addressed to Elana Kobczyk caught her eye, standing out with its festive cheer. A smile touched her lips as she slid it out from the rest.

The warmth inside the house welcomed her immediately, chasing away the chill from her bones. Elana hung her coat and placed the groceries on the counter before settling down at the kitchen table with the mysterious envelope. Her curiosity piqued, she tore it open, expecting a typical Christmas greeting. Instead, another envelope lay inside, this one plain and unassuming, addressed to 'John Kobczyk.' Her brow furrowed at the formal use of her brother's full surname—a name seldom used since his days in the military.

At the top corner of the inner envelope, a handwritten note from Arthur read, *"Elana, Merry Christmas! Please give this to John."* The casual nature of the message belied its serious undertone. Elana knew Arthur, John's old boss from his days with the Office of Strategic Services (OSS) — a connection from a past life John rarely spoke about.

Later that evening, the kitchen of the Kobczyk home was filled with the rich aroma of coffee. Elana had set the table with two coffee cups, anticipating her brother's return. It was their little ritual, a moment of peace in the evening where they could share each other's company, if only for a little while.

John arrived just as the clock chimed seven, stomping off the snow from his boots and coffee cake in his hand, John hung up his thick coat by the door. His face lit up at the sight of the table set for their evening coffee, a welcomed constant in his otherwise unpredictable life.

"Smells wonderful, Elana," he commented as he took his usual seat, his eyes briefly catching the envelope lying next to his plate. *"Arthur's handwriting, isn't it?"*

Elana nodded, pushing the envelope towards him. *"He sent your mail here again. It came inside a Christmas card. Odd way to deliver something so formal, don't you think?"*

John's expression sobered as he picked up the envelope, turning it over in his hands. *"Yes, I did quit working for them,"* he murmured, more to himself than in answer to her unasked question. *"Let's see what's on his mind now. Maybe it's just an invitation for a Christmas party."*

But his sister noticed the slight tension in his shoulders as he spoke, the way his jaw set a little tighter. She knew better. John had left the world of espionage behind—or so he claimed. Yet, something as simple as an envelope from an old officer could stir the shadows of his past, calling to him with a voice he found hard to ignore.

"Aren't you going to read it?" Elana asked after a pause, her voice laced with concern.

John glanced at her, a half-smile playing on his lips, though his eyes remained guarded. *"Yes, in private. You know this is confidential."*

Elana nodded, though dissatisfaction knitted her brow. She poured the coffee, the rich, dark liquid steaming as it hit the cups. *"Always secrets with you, John. Ever since you came back from the war."*

John picked up his cup, the warmth from the coffee seeping into his hands. *"Some secrets keep us safe, Elana. You know that."*

They fell into an easier conversation then, talking about neighbors, family recipes, and the upcoming church bazaar. Yet, the presence of the envelope lingered between them, an unspoken reminder of the life John had tried to leave behind.

Later that night, in the solitude of his own room, John sat at his desk, the envelope lying unopened before him. He lit a cigarette, the smoke curling up towards the ceiling in lazy spirals. His mind raced with possibilities, with fears and what-ifs. With a sudden decisive motion, he tore the envelope open, extracting the single sheet of paper within.

"Merry Christmas, John," it read in Arthur's familiar scrawl. Below, a simple message: *"Join me after Christmas mass at our spot."*

John leaned back in his chair, the paper trembling slightly in his hand. The call to return was clear, unmistakable. He knew the weight of the decision before him, the balance of his peaceful present against the call of duty from his past. As the smoke from his cigarette filled the room, so too did the shadows of a life he thought he had left behind.

The next day, at the local ice rink, John's thoughts were still muddled with the implications of that note as he oversaw the hockey practice of the Buffalo Bisons. The rink was a welcome distraction, the sharp scrape of skates and the crisp slap of pucks against the ice grounding him in the present. Yet, as he leaned against the barrier, clipboard in hand, his gaze was drawn repeatedly to the bleachers.

A figure, cloaked in the anonymity of a dark coat and a lowered hat brim, sat isolated from the few other spectators. Even from this distance, John's trained eyes caught the subtle yet deliberate attempt to blend in, the slight stiffening every time he glanced their way. Memories of covert operations, of being both the watcher and the watched prickled at the back of his neck.

Throughout the practice, John kept the team focused, his commands sharp, a distraction from the unease that tugged at him. But his attention was split, tracking the movements of the mysterious observer as much as the play on the ice. When practice wrapped up and the players dispersed, John's eyes flicked back to the spot. It was empty. The figure had vanished, leaving no trace, no clue but a lingering suspicion in John's mind.

In the days leading up to Christmas, John tried to immerse himself in the festive spirit. His home was adorned with lights and garlands, a tree stood decorated in the living room, and the scent of mulled spices often filled the air. Yet the shadow of that unobserved stranger lingered, coloring his mood with shades of gray.

The bakery was a hive of activity, with the community's demand for holiday treats keeping the ovens hot and counters busy. John found solace in the routine of baking, the precise measurements and the rhythmic kneading of dough. It was during one such busy afternoon, amid the chatter of customers and the clanging of baking trays, that he saw him again.

The man from the rink walked past the bakery window, pausing to peer inside briefly. John's hand tightened around a tray of pastries, his eyes locking with the stranger’s for an electrifying moment before the man moved on. The brief encounter left John's heart pounding, a mix of adrenaline and an old, familiar dread settling in his stomach.

The sighting was no coincidence. John knew the world of espionage well enough to recognize surveillance when he saw it. The question was why? Why now, after years of living quietly, would his past reach out through Arthur's note and this mysterious figure to pull him back into the shadows?

That evening, as John closed up the bakery, the festive lights of the street seemed to mock his growing unease. He walked home with a vigilant eye, scanning the faces of passersby, watching for that familiar stranger among the crowd. But the streets offered up no further clues, just the merry laughter of families and the soft fall of snow.

In his study later that night, the envelope lay open on his desk, Arthur's note a tangible connection to a world John had tried to leave behind. He sat there in the quiet, wrestling with the decision. To meet Arthur was to step back into the fray, to re-engage with a life that had cost him dearly. Yet, as the shadows deepened and the night wore on, a resolve formed within the depths of his being. If his past was reaching out to him, then it was not done with him yet—and he was not done with it.

With a deep, steadying breath, John crushed the cigarette in his ashtray. He would go to the meeting, he decided. He would face Arthur and whatever ghosts his old life brought with it. As he stood, he decided that he would be the one commanding the shadows, not being haunted by them.

Chapter 2: Briefing

He pulled on his coat, feeling its familiar weight settle around him like armor. The fabric, though worn, carried the scent of past winters—each thread intertwined with memories both bitter and sweet.

As John steered his car through the nighttime streets of Buffalo, the hum of the engine mixed uneasily with the whirl of his own conflicted thoughts. Each streetlight that passed overhead briefly illuminated the interior of the car, highlighting the deep furrows of concern etched across John's brow. He was heading towards a rendezvous that felt more like a summons back to a world he had hoped to leave behind—back to espionage, back to the covert existence defined by shadows and secrecy.

Each mile marker ticked by like a countdown to his old life. The decision to meet Arthur wasn't just a step back into the field; it was a plunge into cold waters, a return to a life of concealed identities and hidden agendas. Despite the resolve he had mustered earlier, doubt crept in like the winter chill seeping through the car's seams.

The city lights blurred past, each one seeming to echo his wavering thoughts. *"Am I still that man?"* he wondered, the question looping in his mind like a refrain. "Can I still walk that tightrope between duty and danger?" The comfort of his recent life, the simplicity of routine and the warmth of family gatherings, seemed worlds away from the clandestine meetings and the ever-present threat of betrayal.

As the city's outskirts gave way to the secluded meeting spot, the stark, leafless trees lining the road seemed like sentinels, watching his progress. John's grip tightened on the steering wheel, a physical manifestation of his readiness to face whatever lay ahead. The chill in the air was sharp as he pulled into the parking lot of the Bethlehem Steel Plant, an area that seemed to exist away from the rest of the world—a perfect tableau for conversations that were meant to remain hidden in this 24/7 molten city.

Parking the car, John's eyes immediately found Arthur's vehicle, a lone figure waiting within. The scene was stark, almost surreal under the pale glow of the steel plant. It was here, in this no-man's land between past allegiance and present duty, that John would step back into the shadows. Not as a puppet, but as a puppeteer, ready to command the dance of espionage that awaited him.

Taking a deep breath, John stepped out of his car, the crunch of gravel underfoot grounding him back to reality. He approached the vehicle, each step a definitive beat in the rhythm of his renewed purpose. As he opened the passenger door and greeted Arthur Phillips, his old boss, it wasn't just a meeting of two former colleagues; rather, that of master and apprentice, each aware of the stakes that lay before them. *"How have you been, my friend?"* John asked, his voice steady despite the unease that fluttered in his gut.

"I'm good, John, and you?" Arthur replied, his demeanor belying the tension that lay just beneath his calm exterior. As a peace offering, or perhaps a prelude to less pleasant discussions, he handed John a bottle of Black Velvet whisky. *"Merry Christmas, buddy,"* he said, the festive greeting clashing with the seriousness soon to follow.

John tucked the bottle beside him, nodding his thanks, his senses sharpening as he noted the shift in Arthur's posture—the squared shoulders, the way his hands gripped the steering wheel a little too tightly. *"John, we have a problem,"* Arthur stated plainly, cutting through the pleasantries with a precision that was all too familiar.

John exhaled slowly, the warmth of his breath fogging up the window beside him. *"No, you have a problem, and you need me to fix it, don't you?"* he countered, his tone laced with a mild frustration and a resignation to the fact that his holiday season was about to be overtaken by something much darker than winter snow.

Arthur's gaze met John's, steady and unblinking. *"We've lost two men. We know the city, but we need a location. We can't go to the embassy with this; we can't tell them we just lost two men who have been spying on what we believe are weapons labs. Can you help us?"* His voice was low, each word measured and heavy with the gravity of their situation.

John leaned back against the seat, his mind racing through the potential dangers and the geopolitical chessboard on which they were mere pawns. The weight of his decision pressed down on him, a burden he had borne many times before, yet never with ease. *"Nearly three years of watching these Russians,"* Arthur continued, his voice a mix of weariness and urgency. *"Moving their nuclear engineers and equipment. We have to see what they are doing."*

As the conversation shifted toward the specifics of the mission, John's brows furrowed in concern. *"How does this involve me?"* he asked, struggling to see his place in the unfolding scenario.

Arthur leaned forward, his voice dropping to a conspiratorial whisper, as if the walls of the car themselves might be listening. *"Before our last man was taken, he led us to a small village in the middle of nowhere. Then they go and put up an ice rink! Our U2's confirmed it. But we can't keep putting that much attention on this location without tipping them off. It's a city called Kirov."*

Arthur paused, ensuring John was following. *"A hockey team is using half of its facility; we believe the other side isn't a rink, but an engineering lab. They may have a way to chill small samples and work there under everyone's nose."*

The revelation struck a chord with John. The unusual nature of such a facility hiding in plain sight was exactly the kind of Soviet cunning he had been trained to unearth and dismantle.

Seeing the connection click, Arthur pressed on, tapping into John's past to draw him deeper. *"Since you spent time playing for the Bisons, you, my friend, are a perfect fit. Also, we've got a trigger guy that will be tracking you. He will present himself when he deems the time is right."*

John's expression hardened as he processed the information. The world of espionage was one of shadows and ghosts, of moves and countermoves. *"I can give three weeks, a month maybe,"* he said, thinking aloud. *"Just work your way in like we used to. Let them start seeing your face and interact. You will know when to make your move when the coach disappears. The trigger man will then be your point of contact."*

The mention of the trigger man brought a new layer of complexity to the assignment. John turned to Arthur; curiosity mixed with a hint of apprehension. *"So, who is this trigger man?"* he inquired, needing to know more about the figure who would be his shadow in this dangerous dance.

Arthur's eyes narrowed slightly, the gravity of the situation reflected in his gaze. *"Oh, they call him the silent hornet,"* he replied, his voice a mix of respect and wariness. *"It's said he can take out a target from so far away they never hear the gun before he stings them. The guy lives for this type of work. He's not cut out for your level of delicate work. He just wants to squeeze the trigger on a given target, but you are subtle and can handle a difficult situation."*

The description offered a stark contrast between the trigger man's brute approach and John's need for finesse and discretion. John understood the implications: while the trigger man was a necessary safeguard, his presence was also a reminder of the deadly stakes at play.

As the engine of the car hummed in the background, a silence fell between the two men. It was a heavy silence, filled with the weight of what was being asked of John and what it might cost him. This mission would not just be a test of his skills but also of his resolve and his ability to navigate the murky waters of espionage where every friend could be a foe and every fact a potential fiction.

John looked out the window at the snow-dusted streets, a world away from the dark corners of Kirov where his next mission awaited. His mind was already turning, plotting, planning. The game was set, the pieces were moving, and he was, once again, right at the center of it.

As the briefing drew to a close in the confined space of the car, the atmosphere thickened with the gravity of what lay ahead. Arthur's demeanor shifted, his usual composed self-giving way to a more somber, paternal tone. He fixed John with a steady, meaningful look. *"Remember to stay sharp. They already took two of my men. As always, don't trust one of them, John!"* The warning was stern, a clear reminder of the dangers of espionage where trust was a luxury few could afford.

John absorbed the weight of Arthur's words, the reality of the peril he was stepping back into settling over him. He nodded slowly, a silent affirmation of his understanding and acceptance. Sensing the meeting was nearing its end, Arthur asked, *"Any questions?"* aiming to clear any doubts before they parted ways.

John, with a sly grin cutting through the tension, decided to lighten the mood for a moment. *"Yes. Which one did you like?"* he queried; his tone playful yet probing.

Arthur, momentarily confused by the shift, furrowed his brow. *"Which what did I like?"* he responded, genuinely puzzled.

"Did you like the pastry or the practice on Saturday? I know that was you," John revealed, a glint of mischief in his

eyes but with a serious undertone, confirming his suspicion that Arthur had been observing him recently.

Arthur's expression then morphed into one of approval, a slight smile playing at the corners of his mouth. *"Good. I was just checking if you were still that guy I knew fighting those Germans,"* he admitted, a note of relief in his voice. The test wasn't just about skills—it was about John's readiness, his mental sharpness.

John chuckled softly, the ice between them broken. *"So?"* he prompted, looking for final confirmation.

"You're here, aren't you?" Arthur concluded with a rhetorical question that underscored the point of their meeting. They then shook hands, their grips firm and meaningful, a silent acknowledgment of the risks and weight of the mission John was about to undertake.

As John drove home from the meeting, the festive lights of Buffalo blurred past his car windows. The vibrant decorations and the joyful ambiance of the holiday season stood in stark contrast to the dark currents running through his mind. The conversation with Arthur replayed in his head, each warning and piece of advice embedding itself deeper. The city's festive glow could not pierce the veil of gravity that had settled over him.

During the drive, John wrestled with the decision he had just solidified. The mission's urgency overshadowed the holiday cheer, a sobering reminder of the responsibilities he carried. He knew deep down that no one else possessed the unique combination of skills and experience necessary to navigate this perilous landscape as effectively as he could. More than duty, there was a point to prove—to himself and to those who doubted. Despite the years, despite the desire for a quieter life, he was still capable, still the sharp operative Arthur relied upon.

As he parked his car outside his home, the warmth of the family gathering inside awaited him, a stark contrast to the cold mission ahead. With a deep breath, he prepared himself to hide his mission and departure. To free himself of worried glances of loved ones. More importantly and with ease John keeps his work classified. This mission wasn't just another assignment; it was a test of his enduring capabilities and a dive back into the deep waters of international espionage. John stepped out of the car, his resolve firm, ready to embrace his role, no matter the personal cost. John never thought he'd be spending the beginning of 1959 in the USSR. Buffalo had been perfect for this Polish born boy who works hard and enjoys the comfort of living in the heart of this devoted Polish community.

Chapter 3: Departure

John stepped into the warmth of his home. On the television, "The Bishop's Wife" played softly, the annual Christmas tradition filling the room with its familiar comfort. John smiled despite himself - Elana never tired of watching Cary Grant's charming angel, and he had to admit, Loretta Young's luminous presence always caught his eye. Elana glanced up from her place by the fire, where she had been enjoying the Christmas party, her face lighting up with a welcoming smile. The smile faded slightly as she caught the seriousness in John's expression. She knew that look—she had seen it too many times over the years. It was the look of a man burdened by responsibilities far beyond the ordinary, a man on the brink of departure.

After the party, John crossed the room and sat down beside her, his gaze steady but softened with the affection he held for his sister. He took her hand gently, feeling the warmth of her skin against the coldness that had settled into his bones. *"Elana,"* he began, his voice calm but heavy with the weight of what he had to say, *"I've been called back. There's an assignment, and I have to go."*

"How long?" she asked, her voice barely above a whisper, not wanting to disturb the fragile peace they had in these last few hours together.

"Could be weeks, maybe more. I don't know for sure," John replied, his tone measured, offering no false hope.

Elana nodded slowly, her face a mask of understanding tinged with worry. *"Just be safe Jonny"* she said, her voice steady but carrying the weight of too many farewells.

John managed a brief smile, the kind that was meant to reassure but fell short. *"I'll do my best,"* he replied, knowing full well that safety was never guaranteed in his line of work.

With nothing more to say, John gave her hand a gentle squeeze before standing up. He paused for a moment, taking in the warmth of the room, the quiet strength of his sister. Then, without another word, he turned and made his way to his room, the silence of the house closing in around him as he prepared for the unknown journey ahead.

The evening before his departure was draped in solitude and silence, broken only by the soft shuffle of fabric and the methodical click of a suitcase lock. John Kobczyk stood over his open suitcase laid out on the bed, each fold of his clothing meticulous, a practiced ritual from years of having to pack and unpack in numerous shadow-filled corners of the world. His fingers lingered on the cold metal of his service medals, hidden beneath a layer of shirts. They were stark reminders of a past painted with both honor and secrets, each engraved with memories of missions that were never spoken of outside coded debriefings. Nearby, his old passport—a document that had opened borders and facilitated escapes—sat snugly between the folds of a heavy woolen sweater.

In these quiet moments, John's bedroom felt like a sanctuary of dim light and encroaching shadows. The walls, lined with faded photographs of family and friends, watched silently as he prepared to step back into a life that demanded as much as it dared. The suitcase clicked shut, its sound a definitive note in the otherwise hushed room.

Dawn brought a chill that seeped through the walls of the Kobczyk home. Downstairs in the kitchen, the aroma of brewing coffee and frying bacon wrestled with the underlying tension. Elana Kobczyk moved around the kitchen; her actions automatic as she prepared what she deemed a fortifying breakfast. The skillet hissed, a counterpoint to the heavier sighs that escaped her as she glanced repeatedly towards the staircase, waiting for John to appear.

When he finally did, descending with a quietness that was almost stealthy, Elana's heart clenched tighter. The kitchen, usually a place of warm chatter, was thick with unspoken fears today. She plated the eggs and bacon with a precision that betrayed her nervousness.

"Smells good, Elana," John remarked, managing a tight smile as he took his seat. The normalcy of the gesture, so typical of any other day, was a stark contrast to the gravity of his impending departure.

"Eat up. You'll need your strength," Elana replied, her voice steady but her hands betraying her worry with their slight tremor. John nodded, his eyes meeting hers across the table. There was a resilience in his gaze, born of years in the field, but today it was softened by the familial bond that tethered him to the woman who had seen him off to war and secret missions alike.

Their conversation stumbled—a dance of words that skirted around the dangers of his task. *"I'll be careful, I promise,"* John said, reaching across the table to place a reassuring hand over Elana's. His touch was gentle, an anchor in the swirling uncertainty that threatened to engulf them both.

Elana's smile was taut, a facade she wore to mask the fear that gnawed at her insides. *"Just make sure you come back to us, John. That's all I ask."* Her voice was firm, the maternal command that had always sought to protect him, from childhood scrapes to the far more lethal scrapes of his OSS days.

They finished breakfast in a companionable silence that was thick with unsaid goodbyes. John washed his dishes, a mundane act that felt like a ritual farewell to domestic life.

When he turned to leave the kitchen, Elana's hand on his arm stopped him. Her grip was tight, her eyes searching his for a promise—a silent plea for his safe return.

The sudden chime of the doorbell sliced through the quiet atmosphere, a sharp reminder that the time for departure was drawing near. John exhaled softly, a quiet resignation settling over him as he released Elana's hand and made his way to the door. Pulling it open, he was met by the sight of William standing on the stoop of John's well-worn but cherished home. William had been John's closest friend since they were boys, the one person outside of Elana he trusted without question. Through wars and peacetime, William had remained steady as granite, watching over Elana whenever John's duties took him away. The crisp morning air was alive with the threat of snow, a silent yet persistent reminder of the changes both in the weather and in John's life.

John emerged from the doorway, his face set in a mask of determination that didn't quite reach his eyes. William, ever the observer, noted the subtle tension in John's shoulders—a telltale sign of the inner turmoil brewing beneath his calm exterior. As they met at the bottom of the steps, their handshake was firm, lingering, an unspoken testament to the seriousness of the moment.

"Keep close watch over Elana for me, will you?" John's voice was low, almost a whisper, as if the weight of his request might crumble if spoken too loudly. His eyes, usually a fortress

of resolve, betrayed a flicker of vulnerability as he issued his plea.

William nodded, his own expression grave. *"You have my word,"* he assured, his voice thick with the gravity of the promise. The morning chill seemed to deepen, carrying with it the silent acknowledgment of the risks John was about to take, and the responsibility now resting on William's shoulders.

With a final squeeze on John's shoulder, William stepped back, allowing John the space to set forth on his journey. John took in the sight of the home that had been his sanctuary. The early rays of light cast a warm glow through the windows, painting a picture of domestic tranquility that he was leaving behind. His heart tightened at the thought, but the resolve in his stride did not waver.

John’s steps down the path were measured and heavy, each one echoing a mix of resolve and regret. The crisp morning air bit at his skin, a stark contrast to the warmth he was leaving behind. As he reached the car, he allowed himself one last look at the place that had anchored him for so long, then turned resolutely, setting his sights on the uncertain and perilous road ahead.

The Central Terminal train station in Buffalo was a bustling hub of activity, the air vibrating with the sounds of greetings and goodbyes. John moved through the crowd with a practiced ease, his senses sharpened by years of training. His eyes scanned the throng, instinctively categorizing faces and movements, always alert to the undercurrents of danger that might lurk beneath the surface.

At the platform, the noise seemed to crescendo, wrapping around him in a cacophony of human emotion. When he spotted Elana, something tightened within him. Her presence was a bittersweet reminder of what he was protecting—and what he risked losing. As he drew her into a tight embrace, he felt her body tremble slightly against his.

"I'll be back before you know it," he whispered, his voice steady despite the turmoil inside. It was a promise—a vow made not just to comfort her but to steel himself against the daunting path he had chosen.

Elana pulled back, her eyes searching his, looking for the assurance that her heart needed. She managed a nod, her lips pressed into a thin line to hold back the words that might weaken his resolve.

With a final nod to William, who stood a respectful distance away, John turned and mounted the steps to the train. The sliding doors closed behind him with a hiss, sealing him off from his past life and propelling him toward a future fraught with shadows and uncertainty.

Inside the train, John found a seat by the window, his eyes fixed on the receding figures of Elana and William. As the train pulled away from the Buffalo station, John Kobczyk secured the seat, his posture relaxed but his mind sharply attuned to his surroundings. He unfolded a newspaper, its crisp pages a mere prop in the elaborate performance of normalcy he was compelled to adopt. Outside, the world rushed by—a mosaic of barren trees and frost-covered fields, each fading into the other as the train sped on. The rhythmic clatter of the train over the tracks provided a steady soundtrack to his thoughts, each beat a reminder of the distance widening between him and his past life.

John's gaze drifted beyond the glass, but his mind was far from the wintry scenes passing before him. Instead, he revisited the darker landscapes of his previous missions, the memories playing out like scenes from an old film. He saw the shadowed alleyways of Berlin, heard the hushed voices of contacts in dimly lit cafés across Eastern Europe, and felt the adrenaline of narrow escapes that had marked his years in the field. Each recollection was a brushstroke in the complex portrait of his past, highlighting the skills he had honed—surveillance, evasion, deception. Yet, these memories were interspersed with faces of friends who had not made it back, their fates sealed in the silent sacrifices demanded by espionage.

The train's steady pace and the monotony of travel allowed John's senses to heighten, sharpening his awareness as he shifted from reflection to the immediate necessity of vigilance. He began to study his fellow passengers with the practiced eye of a seasoned operative. A couple arguing quietly over a map, a businessman absorbed in his ledger, a young woman lost in the pages of a romance novel—each presented a façade to be deciphered, a potential puzzle piece in the larger mosaic of threats and allies.

John's fingers turned the pages of his newspaper nonchalantly, but his eyes missed nothing. He noted the exits, mentally mapped the layout of the car, and rehearsed escape routes in his mind. His training dictated that preparation was as critical as execution, and even this mundane journey was a field for rehearsal.

As the landscape shifted from the industrial outskirts of American cities to the more refined urban sprawl of New York City, John's journey took him deeper into the realm of his professional resurgence. After a brief layover in the bustling grandeur of New York, he boarded an international flight to Munich—a lengthy transit that carried him over the Atlantic, into the heart of post-war Europe.

Landing in Munich was a jolt back to operational mode. The Cold War's invisible lines crisscrossed through the city, a silent battleground of ideologies and espionage, though here, away from the tense East-West divide of Berlin, the atmosphere was somewhat less guarded. Munich and its surrounding countryside offered a brief respite from the intense scrutiny of more volatile borders, but John knew that caution was still his best ally.

Before continuing his journey, John made his way to a discreet safehouse tucked away in the quieter outskirts of the city. The building was unassuming, a nondescript residence that blended seamlessly into the neighborhood, betraying nothing of the covert operations that took place within its walls. Inside, he was greeted by his point of contact—a fellow agent whose stern professionalism matched the gravity of the mission.

In a dimly lit room, John was handed the necessary documents: a forged passport, entry papers, and the essentials he would need to cross into Soviet-controlled Poland. From this moment on, he would no longer be John Kobczyk. The papers bore his new identity—***Andrei Novikov***, a name that carried with it a heavy burden of responsibility and the weight of the mission ahead. The agent, a man of few words, also provided him with a modest car, ensuring he could approach the border under the guise of a routine traveler. "Everything you need is here. Once you cross, you're on your own," the agent said, his tone flat but laced with the implicit understanding of the risks Andrei was about to face.

With the new documents safely tucked away, Andrei left the safehouse, the relative calm of Munich already fading as he set out for the border. The drive through the countryside was quiet, the lower risks of this region allowing him to focus on the road ahead, but as he neared the Polish border, the stakes rose once again. Each border crossing heightened the tension, the invisible eyes of border guards measuring each passenger with a scrutiny born of tense geopolitical realities.

Settling into his seat on the train that would take him further east, Andrei casually glanced at his watch, a movement timed and precise. He counted the seconds, watching through his peripheral vision to see if any fellow passenger mirrored his action—a simple yet effective trick to identify if he was under surveillance. This subtle dance of watchfulness was a testament to the nuances of his trade, where even the smallest gesture could unveil a pursuer.

Each time his small test confirmed his safety, Andrei's shoulders relaxed fractionally, only to tense again as the next potential observer entered his field of view. The countryside of Europe sped by his window, a blur of greens and browns, quaint villages and sprawling fields soon giving way to the more austere landscapes of Eastern Europe.

As the train crossed the Polish border, the reality of his mission pressed ever closer. The once-familiar thrill of the chase, the espionage dance he had once excelled in, now carried a weight he had not anticipated when he first agreed to Arthur's request. Andrei's hand went to his watch again, his glance quick and practiced. This time, his reflection in the window caught his eye—a man marked by years and experiences, shaped by both victories and losses, now riding the rails into uncertain territory under a new name and identity.

Chapter 4:
Arrival in Europe

The train's whistle cut through the early morning mist as it slowly rolled into the station, the screech of metal-on-metal echoing off the rugged, snow-dusted platform. John Kobczyk stared out the window as the train lurched to a halt, taking in the scene that unfolded before him. The small Polish station, with its soot-streaked walls and aging architecture, was a stark contrast to the bustling European cities he had passed through earlier. Yet, there was something about it that felt oddly comforting, a familiarity rooted deep in his memory.

John inhaled deeply, the distinct scent of coal smoke and damp earth filling his lungs. It was the smell of his childhood, the smell of a place where the world had once been simpler, before war and duty had dragged him across continents and into the shadowy corners of international intrigue. But that comfort was tempered by a sharp awareness—this was no longer just home; this was the Eastern Bloc, a land where allegiances were murky and every interaction could mask hidden dangers.

As John stepped off the train, the cold air bit at his face, a sharp reminder of the harsh realities that awaited him. His senses were immediately on high alert, every instinct honed by years of training kicking in. The worn faces of the villagers going about their morning routines told a story of endurance, of lives lived under the weight of history. But John wasn't just seeing the village as a returning native; he was seeing it as an operative, where each familiar sight was tinged with the possibility of threat.

John adjusted his grip on his bag and began walking across the platform, his steps purposeful yet unhurried. As he moved through the small crowd, his eyes scanned the scene with the casual ease of someone merely observing his surroundings, but every detail was meticulously cataloged. He noticed the way the villagers moved, their expressions, their interactions—seeking out anything that seemed out of place.

That's when he saw him. A man, seemingly engrossed in a newspaper, stood near the station entrance. He was too deliberate in his stillness, too focused on blending in while his eyes flicked up every so often, tracking John's movements. John felt a familiar prickle at the back of his neck, a silent warning that he was being watched. The man's gaze lingered a fraction too long, his posture too stiff, his presence too contrived.

John didn't alter his pace, but his mind quickly ran through the possibilities. Was this man a Soviet agent? A local informant? Or perhaps someone even more dangerous, embedded in the village for reasons that had nothing to do with

John's mission? Without missing a step, John made a quick decision to test his observer.

He casually adjusted his path, heading towards a different exit, one less used by the main flow of passengers. The man hesitated, his newspaper dropping slightly as he seemed to consider his options. Then, almost imperceptibly, he shifted and began to follow, confirming John's suspicion that this was no ordinary passerby.

John's pulse quickened, but his exterior remained calm, almost indifferent. Blending into the crowd, he quickened his pace slightly, weaving between the clusters of villagers, moving with the practiced ease of someone who had done this a thousand times before. He glanced briefly over his shoulder, catching the man still trailing him, his expression now more focused, more determined.

John made a sharp turn down a narrow alley that ran alongside the station—a shortcut he remembered from his youth, back when he had played in these very streets. The alley was cramped and shadowed, with uneven cobblestones underfoot and damp, moss-covered walls on either side. It wasn't the best escape route, but it was familiar, and he needed to buy himself some time.

He darted around a corner and paused, pressing his back against the cold, rough stone of a building, his breath held as he listened. The soft sound of footsteps echoed faintly, growing closer. John's muscles tensed, his mind calculating the best course of action. He couldn't afford a confrontation here, not so close to his destination, and certainly not without knowing who he was up against.

The footsteps halted just before the corner, and John knew the man was considering his next move. After a tense moment, the sound of retreating steps reached John's ears, the man evidently deciding to abandon the pursuit rather than risk exposure. John waited a few more seconds before cautiously peeking around the corner, confirming that the alley was now empty.

With the immediate danger passed, John resumed his journey, his mind already processing the encounter, analyzing it from every angle. Whoever that man was, he hadn't been expecting John to notice him so quickly. It was a small victory, but it reminded John that his instincts were still sharp, even after years of trying to leave this life behind.

Leaving the station behind, John made his way through the familiar landscape of his youth. The road to his aunt's village was lined with modest homes, the kind where the paint had long since peeled, and the roofs sagged under the weight of time and snow. Old trees, their branches bare and skeletal, cast long shadows across the dirt paths that wound between the fields. The village hadn't changed much since he was a boy—perhaps a few new faces, a few more empty homes, but the essence of it remained the same.

When John finally reached his aunt's cottage, he paused for a moment, taking in the sight. The small, weathered house stood like a sentinel against the encroaching wilderness, its facade marked by years of wind and rain. A single light shone in the window, a beacon of warmth in the otherwise cold and indifferent world.

John approached the door, his heart heavy with both anticipation and unease. The life he was about to reenter here was worlds apart from the one he had just narrowly escaped at the station. Yet, they were inextricably linked—his past and present, the peaceful and the perilous.

He knocked softly, almost hesitant to break the quiet. When the door opened, and he saw his aunt's familiar face, the years melted away in an instant. She looked older, frailer than he remembered, but the fire in her eyes was the same. They stood there for a moment, just looking at each other.

"John!" she exclaimed, her voice trembling slightly, more from emotion than age. She reached out with frail, shaking hands, pulling him into a warm embrace. The hug was tight but gentle, as if she was holding onto a piece of her past that had suddenly come back to life. John, who had seen so much death and deceit, felt a pang of guilt at the comfort he found in her arms. He was struck by how much she had aged—her once sturdy frame now fragile, her hair thinner and whiter than he remembered. Yet, the strength that had carried her through two world wars still radiated from her.

“It's been too long,” John murmured, his voice thick with unspoken emotions. He pulled back slightly, taking in her appearance, the lines of worry and wear etched deeply into her face.

“Too long indeed,” she replied, her smile never wavering. She motioned him inside, and as John crossed the threshold, the warmth of the small cottage enveloped him. The comforting scent of homemade soup filled the air, mingling with the familiar mustiness of a house that had weathered many winters. The fire crackled in the hearth, its light casting dancing shadows on the walls.

As John took off his coat and hung it by the door, he glanced around the room. The cottage was just as he remembered—modest, but filled with the trappings of a life lived simply and fully. Old photographs lined the mantel, their sepia tones capturing moments from a time before the world had gone mad. Hand-stitched quilts adorned the backs of the chairs, each one a piece of family history, stitched together with love and endurance.

They sat down at the small, worn wooden table, where his aunt had already set out bowls of steaming soup. As they ate, the familiarity of the surroundings grounded John, pulling him out of the shadows of his mission, if only for a moment. The years melted away, and for a brief time, he was simply a nephew visiting his beloved aunt, far removed from the world of espionage and danger.

His aunt broke the silence, her voice carrying the weight of years gone by. “The world has changed so much, John,” she began, her tone reflective. “But some things never change. The struggles, the sacrifices—our family has seen it all.” She paused, taking a sip of soup before continuing. “I remember the first war, how it tore everything apart. And then the second, when we thought we couldn’t endure any more, but we did.”

John listened intently, the rhythm of her words pulling him into the past, into stories he had heard before but now understood in a different light. She spoke of the hardships they had endured—the rationing, the fear, the loss of loved ones. Her voice was steady, but the sorrow in her eyes betrayed the deep pain she carried.

“We lost so many,” she said quietly, her gaze drifting to the photographs on the mantel. “But we also found strength in each other, in the family. That’s what kept us going. And that’s why you’re here, isn’t it, John? To keep fighting for what’s left?”

John didn’t respond immediately. Instead, he looked down at his hands, rough from years of work, both honest and covert. His aunt’s words stirred something deep within him—a reminder of why he had chosen this life, why he continued to fight. It wasn’t just for duty or country, but for the people who had given him everything, who had survived so much just to see another day.

"Yes," John finally replied, his voice firm. "I'm here to protect what's left. To make sure that what happened to us never happens again."

His aunt reached across the table, her hand resting on his. "You've always been strong, John. But remember, strength isn't just in the fight. It's in knowing when to hold on and when to let go."

The words lingered in the air as they finished their meal in companionable silence. The fire crackled softly, casting a warm glow over the room, as if to ward off the cold realities that lay beyond the walls of the cottage.

After dinner, as the afternoon deepened and the air grew colder, his aunt suggested they visit the family grave sites. John agreed, knowing that this was not just a visit, but a pilgrimage—a reminder of the lives that had been lost, and the duty that had been passed down to him.

They walked together through the village, the snow crunching softly under their boots. The cemetery was a quiet, somber place, tucked away at the edge of the village, surrounded by tall, bare trees that swayed gently in the wind. The gravestones were old, many of them weathered and worn, the names barely legible.

As they stood before the graves of his parents and other relatives, John felt a surge of emotions—grief, anger, and a deep, burning sense of injustice. These were the people who had given him life, who had shaped him into the man he was today. And they had been taken by the same forces he now fought against. His hands clenched into fists at his sides, the cold biting into his skin as his anger simmered beneath the surface.

But as quickly as the anger came, it was channeled into something more productive—determination. A renewed resolve to protect what remained, to honor the memory of those who had been lost by ensuring that their sacrifices were not in vain.

His aunt, sensing his turmoil, placed a hand on his shoulder, her touch gentle but grounding. "They're watching over you, John. You carry their strength with you. Don't ever forget that."

John nodded, swallowing the lump in his throat. "I won't," he promised, his voice barely above a whisper.

As they turned to leave, the weight of his mission pressed down on him once more, but this time it was tempered by the knowledge that he wasn't alone. He carried the strength of his family, their history, their sacrifices, with him. And that was something no enemy could ever take away.

As they walked back to the cottage, the world around John seemed sharper, more defined. The cold air was invigorating now, a stark contrast to the warmth of his resolve. He knew the path ahead would be fraught with danger, but he was ready. The mission was no longer just about duty; it was personal.

Later that evening, they sat together in the small, cozy living room, the fire crackling softly as its flickering light cast long shadows on the walls. The warmth was a welcome relief from the outside chill, but John's mind was already shifting gears, moving from the personal to the professional.

He began to ask his aunt subtle questions, his tone casual as he inquired about the recent happenings in the area. "Have you noticed anything unusual around the village? Any new faces, perhaps?"

His aunt, unaware of the true intent behind his questions, nodded thoughtfully. "There have been strangers in town recently, asking questions. And there's been more military activity nearby than usual—trucks coming and going at odd hours."

John's heart rate quickened, though he kept his expression neutral. Each piece of information was a potential clue, a puzzle piece he would need to fit together when the time was right. He listened carefully, storing away every detail. The signs were subtle, but they were there—indicators that something was happening in this quiet corner of the world, something that could lead him to the missing agents.

As the conversation continued, John's mind worked rapidly, piecing together the information his aunt had unwittingly provided. This wasn't just a visit to reconnect with his past; it was the beginning of his mission, and the clues he gathered here could be the key to unlocking the secrets he needed to uncover.

Just after a few moments, his aunt broke the silence.

"John," she began hesitantly, "I noticed something in your papers. Your name—it wasn't yours."

John paused, then set his cup down. "They've given me a new identity. For the mission, I'm Andrei Novikov."

His aunt nodded slowly, absorbing this. "It's strange, but necessary," she said. "Whatever name you go by, remember who you are."

"I will," John—now Andrei—promised, the weight of her words settling in.

Later, as they parted for the night, she softly said, "Good night, Andrei."

Andrei smiled, a final acknowledgment of the man he had to become. "Good night."

He closed the door, the cottage now holding memories of John Kobczyk, while Andrei Novikov prepared for a journey ahead towards Kirov to face the mission ahead.

Chapter 5:

Shadows of the Past

The journey to Kirov was a blur of cold, distant landscapes and fleeting thoughts of what he was leaving behind. As the train carried him deeper into the Soviet Union, Andrei felt the familiar tension of a mission begin to coil within him, tightening with each mile. By the time the train began to slow, the weight of his new identity had fully settled on his shoulders, and the transition from John to Andrei was complete.

The train's brakes hissed as it slowed to a stop at Kirov's small, dimly lit station. Andrei Novikov, once known as John Kobczyk, stood from his seat, pulling his bag from the overhead rack with a steady hand. His heart, however, was anything but calm. As he moved towards the exit, the unveiling of his new identity settled heavy on his shoulders. Every step closer to the platform was a step deeper into the Soviet Union, into the lion's den.

The cold air of Kirov hit him as he stepped off the train, biting at his face and hands. The station was stark, its walls gray and worn, the remnants of an era of harsh utilitarianism. Around him, guards and officers milled about, their eyes sharp, scanning each passenger with practiced suspicion. Andrei kept his expression neutral, careful not to draw any unnecessary attention as he moved forward, merging with the flow of disembarking travelers.

He approached the border officer's desk with measured steps. The officer, a stout man with a stern face, barely glanced up as Andrei handed over his forged documents. Andrei's heart pounded in his chest, but his face remained composed, his breathing steady. The officer flipped through the pages, pausing briefly at the photograph before looking up, his eyes locking onto Andrei's with a cold intensity.

Andrei met the gaze without flinching, forcing his thoughts to slow down, to focus. He had rehearsed this moment countless times, the careful crafting of a backstory, the subtle adjustment of his accent. Everything rode on this moment. The officer's eyes narrowed slightly before he finally stamped the passport and handed it back, nodding for Andrei to proceed.

Andrei gave a polite nod in return, his voice steady as he thanked the officer in flawless Russian. He turned and walked away, resisting the urge to glance back. He allowed himself to exhale only when he was clear of the station, the tension in his shoulders easing just slightly. He had passed the first test, but the real challenge was just beginning.

Once inside Kirov, Andrei fully embraced the role of Novikov. The city, shrouded in the gray gloom of winter, was a labyrinth of old streets and oppressive buildings. Andrei moved through it with purpose, his demeanor that of a man comfortable in his surroundings. His accent, carefully practiced, now rolled off his tongue with ease as he engaged with the locals. He attended a welcome dinner hosted by city officials, where he met the people from the hockey federation.

The dinner was held in a grand but austere hall, the long table lined with Soviet officials and local dignitaries. The conversation was formal, peppered with subtle political undertones. Andrei spoke only when necessary, offering polite but vague responses, always careful to align his words with his cover story. He listened intently, picking up on the nuances of their speech, the underlying tension in their words. Each gesture, each phrase, was calculated to reinforce his identity as Andrei Novikov—a Polish coach with a deep appreciation for Soviet sports culture.

As the evening wore on, Andrei navigated the social interactions with precision. He made sure to be seen as friendly yet reserved, a man focused on his work rather than on the political machinations around him. The officials seemed satisfied with their new guest, their initial scrutiny gradually giving way to a more relaxed atmosphere. By the time the dinner ended, Andrei had successfully blended into the fabric of Kirov's society, a ghost from another life now fully embodied in a new identity.

After the dinner, Andrei was escorted to his assigned apartment. The building was nondescript, a blocky structure typical of Soviet architecture, designed more for function than comfort. The apartment itself was small and sparsely furnished, its plain walls and simple furniture offering little in the way of personality. Andrei stepped inside, closing the door behind him with a quiet click. The room was silent, except for the faint hum of the city outside.

He moved through the space with deliberate caution, his eyes scanning every corner, every shadow. The windows were covered with thick curtains, the kind that could block both light and prying eyes. He checked the exits, noting their positions and the quickest routes to them. The placement of furniture, the angle of the doors—all were carefully observed, memorized. Andrei unpacked his bag methodically, arranging his belongings in a way that suggested he was settling in for a long stay. Yet, his mind never strayed far from the mission at hand.

The next morning, Andrei set out to explore Kirov under the guise of getting to know the city. The streets were bustling with activity, the local population going about their daily routines. But beneath the surface, there was a palpable tension, a sense of underlying control that permeated every aspect of life here.

Andrei walked with purpose, his gaze sweeping over the landmarks, the key locations he would need to familiarize himself with. He made mental notes of the terrain, the layout of the streets, the placement of government buildings. As he passed by the local ice rink, his pace slowed subtly. The rink was a large, utilitarian structure, its exterior giving little away. Andrei watched as players and coaches moved in and out, his eyes catching the details—security measures, the number of entrances, the patterns of movement.

He continued walking, his demeanor that of a curious visitor, but his mind was working rapidly. The ice rink was more than just a sports facility—of that he was certain. The challenge would be uncovering what lay beneath the surface, hidden behind the facade of Soviet sportsmanship.

As he returned to his apartment later that day, Andrei's thoughts were already turning over the possibilities, the clues he had gathered in these early hours. The mission was beginning to take shape, the pieces slowly falling into place. But the dangers were also becoming more apparent. Every step in Kirov was a step into the unknown, a delicate dance on the edge of a knife.

Andrei Novikov knew this all too well. John Kobczyk, however, had to stay buried deep beneath the surface, hidden away until the mission was complete.

As the days in Kirov stretched on, Andrei Novikov made a habit of frequenting local cafes and shops, weaving himself into the fabric of the community. Each visit was an opportunity to gather information, and Andrei approached it with the precision of a seasoned operative. The locals, accustomed to new faces coming and going in their town, seemed to accept him without much question. His charm and careful politeness put them at ease, and soon enough, they were chatting with him as if he were one of their own.

Andrei was careful in how he steered conversations. He asked about the town's history, the weather, and the local sports scene, always circling back to the ice rink. The rink, he learned, was more than just a place for hockey—it was a social hub. People from all walks of life passed through its doors, whether to watch games, attend events, or simply meet friends. It was a focal point in the community, a place where the town's heartbeat could be felt most strongly.

In one café, Andrei listened as a group of older men reminisced about the town's glory days, when their local team had made it to the regional championships. The conversation naturally drifted to the present, and one of the men mentioned how much the rink had changed in recent years—more security, fewer public events, and a new group of men who seemed more interested in what happened off the ice than on it. Andrei nodded along, mentally cataloging every detail. The rink was beginning to reveal itself as more than just a sports facility; it was a place where secrets were kept, and where the missing agents might have met their fate.

One evening, after a long day of blending into the town's rhythms, Andrei began the walk back to his apartment. The streets of Kirov were dark and cold, the few streetlights casting long, distorted shadows. It was then that he felt it—a presence, subtle but undeniable. Someone was following him.

Andrei's instincts sharpened, and he slowed his pace slightly, listening for the sound of footsteps behind him. They were there, faint but persistent. Without turning around, Andrei made a quick decision. He altered his route, veering into a side street that was less illuminated. The footsteps followed. The tension mounted, but Andrei's expression remained neutral, his movements unhurried.

He led the follower into a narrow alley, the kind that was more shadow than light, with tall buildings on either side creating a tunnel-like effect. Then, in a swift motion, Andrei ducked into a recessed doorway, pressing himself into the shadows. He held his breath, listening.

The footsteps grew louder, then stopped. Andrei peered out from his hiding place, watching as a figure hesitated in the middle of the alley, scanning the area. The figure's silhouette was indistinct, but the intent was clear—this was no ordinary passerby. After a moment, the figure turned and retreated, melting back into the darkness. Andrei stayed hidden until he was certain the threat had passed, his mind racing with the implications. His cover was still intact, but the net was tightening.

The next day, Andrei returned to the ice rink with renewed vigilance. He attended a practice session, his eyes scanning the crowd, the players, and the staff. His earlier conversations had confirmed that something was off about this place, and Andrei was determined to find out what it was. As he moved through the facility, he noticed a group of men standing off to the side, their attention not on the ice but on something—or someone—else.

These men were different from the others. They didn't cheer or engage with the game. Instead, they huddled together, speaking in low tones, their eyes darting around the rink as if watching for something. Andrei observed them quietly, noting their movements, their interactions. They were careful, but Andrei had seen enough in his career to recognize when something was being concealed.

Later, under the guise of assessing the training conditions, Andrei explored more of the facility. He walked down a corridor that led away from the public areas, his steps echoing in the silence. At the end of the hallway, he found a door that was locked—an area marked off-limits. Andrei paused, his hand hovering over the handle, his mind racing with possibilities. This was the place. Whatever secrets the rink held, they were behind this door.

In the following days, Andrei's careful observations began to pay off. He overheard a conversation between two rink employees discussing a recent delivery that had arrived late at night. The details were vague, but the tone and context suggested something more than just sports equipment. Andrei's heart quickened as he realized this could be the lead he had been waiting for.

Discreetly, he followed up on the conversation, questioning other staff members with the practiced ease of someone just making small talk. The delivery, he learned, had been taken to the restricted area he had noted earlier. This revelation confirmed his suspicions—the ice rink was more than it appeared, and it was directly tied to the fate of the missing agents.

Andrei knew he was getting closer to the truth, but with that knowledge came greater danger. The shadows of Kirov were thickening around him, and the line between hunter and hunted was beginning to blur. The mission was far from over, and every step deeper into the heart of Kirov brought him closer to uncovering a conspiracy that reached further than he had ever imagined.

As Andrei left the ice rink, blending into the flow of the evening crowd, he noticed a man moving with purpose toward a secluded alley. The man glanced around, his movements nervous and hurried. Andrei's instincts kicked in; he recognized the behavior of someone about to make a drop. Keeping a safe distance, Andrei shadowed the man, watching as he slipped a small envelope behind a loose brick in the alley wall before hastily retreating.

Once the man was out of sight, Andrei approached the wall with calculated calm. With a quick, fluid motion, he retrieved the envelope and tucked it into his coat. He continued down the street as if nothing had happened, the envelope's weight a silent reminder of the information it might contain. He would decode it later, in the safety of his apartment.

While heading towards his apartment, Andrei saw a small bakery on the roadside. He pushed open the door to the small bakery, the soft jingle of the bell above announcing his arrival. The warmth of the shop was a welcome relief from the biting cold outside, and the scent of freshly baked bread wrapped around him like a comforting embrace. He stepped inside, allowing the door to close gently behind him, and took a moment to survey the scene.

The bakery was modest, with just a few tables scattered near the windows and shelves lined with golden loaves and pastries. It was the kind of place that felt timeless, untouched by the harshness of the world beyond its walls. Andrei's gaze swept the room, noting the handful of customers quietly enjoying their purchases, but his attention was quickly drawn to the woman behind the counter.

She moved with a grace that seemed out of place in a town like Kirov, her hands deftly wrapping a loaf of bread for an elderly customer. The way she smiled—genuine and warm—caught Andrei off guard. It was a rare thing to see in a place where suspicion and fear were the norms. He lingered near the entrance, watching as she handed the bread to the old man with a gentle nod and a soft word. The man's face softened in response, a flicker of warmth in his eyes as he left the shop, the loaf cradled in his arms like a precious treasure.

Andrei shook off the momentary distraction and stepped forward to the counter. As he approached, the woman looked up, her eyes meeting his. For a brief second, time seemed to slow, and Andrei felt something stir within him—something he hadn't allowed himself to feel in years. He quickly suppressed it, reminding himself of the mission, of the dangers that lurked around every corner.

"Good evening," she greeted him, her voice as warm as her smile. *"What can I get for you?"*

"Just a loaf of bread," Andrei replied, his tone measured, but he couldn't help but notice the subtle lilt in her voice, the way her eyes seemed to hold a depth of kindness that was almost unsettling in its sincerity.

As she wrapped the bread, Andrei studied her, committing every detail to memory—the way she tucked a loose strand of hair behind her ear, the slight furrow of concentration in her brow as she worked. When she handed him the loaf, their fingers brushed briefly, and Andrei felt a spark, a connection that he hadn't expected.

"Thank you," he said, his voice betraying a hint of something more—something he couldn't afford to explore.

"You're welcome," she replied, her eyes lingering on his for a moment before she turned to the next customer.

Andrei left the bakery, the warmth of the shop replaced by the cold reality of the streets. As he walked back to his apartment, the image of the young woman stayed with him, her smile, her kindness—a stark contrast to the world of shadows and deception he had immersed himself in. It stirred memories, pulling him back to a time when he had been John Kobczyk, before the war had hardened him, before duty had consumed every part of who he was.

His mind drifted to the missions that had defined his life. The flashbacks came unbidden, vivid and relentless. He saw himself crawling through the mud under a moonless sky, the sound of enemy patrols just yards away. He remembered the sharp crack of gunfire, the way it echoed through the night as he led his team through a firefight, every decision a matter of life and death. And then there was the moment that haunted him most—the decision that had cost a comrade's life, a choice that had to be made to complete the mission. It was the price of war, the price of survival, but it had left scars that no amount of time could heal.

Andrei shook his head, forcing the memories back into the depths of his mind. He couldn't afford to dwell on the past, not now. The mission in Kirov demanded his full attention, and there was no room for distraction. But the encounter in the bakery lingered, a reminder that there was still a part of him that could feel, that could connect, even in the coldest of places.

Back at his apartment, Andrei settled into his routine. The coded message he had intercepted sat on his desk, waiting for his attention. The room was dimly lit, the only sound the faint hum of the city outside. Andrei sat down, his fingers tracing the edges of the paper before he began the painstaking process of decryption.

His hands moved with the precision of someone who had done this a thousand times before, each symbol, each letter falling into place. The process was methodical, almost meditative, a familiar task in an unfamiliar world. As the code unraveled, Andrei's mind sharpened, the information slowly revealing itself—a fragment of a larger puzzle that he was determined to solve.

Hours passed, the message finally decrypted and analyzed. It contained details about a shipment scheduled to arrive at the ice rink—a shipment that, according to his contact, was far more than just sports equipment. Andrei's instincts told him that this was a lead worth following, but he needed more information, more context before he could act.

The shadows outside had deepened by the time Andrei decided to reach out to an old contact. The man was a former operative, someone who had retired into the shadows of Kirov, living quietly but maintaining connections to the undercurrents of the town. Andrei needed his insight, his knowledge of the local dynamics, and most importantly, his discretion.

Andrei slipped into the night, his steps silent as he made his way to the abandoned warehouse where they had agreed to meet. The air was thick with tension, every sound amplified by the silence of the night. As he approached the building, a figure emerged from the shadows—a man in his late fifties, his face lined with years of experience, his eyes sharp despite his age.

The conversation was brief, but it was enough. Andrei's contact confirmed that the ice rink was indeed the center of something much larger—an operation that involved more than just local players and coaches. The details were still unclear, but the risks were evident. Andrei thanked the man, the exchange ending with a nod, both men aware that they had just crossed a line that couldn't be uncrossed.

As Andrei made his way back to his apartment, his mind raced with possibilities. The ice rink was the key to everything—that much was clear. But how to get closer? How to infiltrate a place that was both a public venue and a private stronghold?

The answer came to him suddenly, a flash of inspiration that felt both dangerous and inevitable. He needed to secure a position as something like an assistant coach. It was the perfect cover—one that would grant him access to the rink regularly, allow him to observe, and gather information without raising suspicion. The role would give him access to areas that might otherwise be off-limits but without drawing too much attention or putting him directly in the limelight. More importantly, it would allow him to move freely within the very heart of the operation.

The decision settled into his mind with a finality that left no room for doubt. As Andrei closed the door to his apartment, the shadows of Kirov seemed to press in around him, but his resolve was firm. Andrei Novikov would join the team, and through it, he would uncover the truth that lay hidden beneath the surface. The mission was far from over, but the path forward had become clear.

With that, the chapter of Andrei Novikov's infiltration deepened, the next steps of his mission were set in motion, the silent darkness of Kirov enveloping him.

Chapter 6:
The KGB's Trial

As dusk crept across Kirov, painting the Soviet city in muted hues of gray and blue. Andrei Novikov, formerly John Kobczyk, sat in his sparsely furnished apartment, the weight of his mission pressing down on him like a physical force. His eyes, sharp and alert despite the late hour, scanned the room for the hundredth time, searching for any sign that his cover had been compromised.

As he sat there, his mind drifted to the challenge ahead. "How am I going to secure a position on the coaching staff?" he muttered to himself, his brow furrowing. The ice rink was key to his mission, but infiltrating it would require more than just his fabricated credentials. He needed a way in, a stroke of luck or a carefully orchestrated opportunity.

Yet, a flicker of doubt crept into his thoughts. Was the lead about the ice rink solid, or was he chasing shadows? The uncertainty gnawed at him, adding another layer of complexity to his already precarious situation. He needed confirmation, some tangible proof that he was on the right track.

Pushing the worry aside for the moment, Andrei reached for the old radio perched on a rickety side table. His fingers, calloused from years of both baking and espionage, carefully adjusted the dial. Static crackled through the air, punctuated by snippets of propaganda and weather reports. Then, suddenly, the melancholic strains of "Lubimiy Gorod" filled the room.

Andrei's breath caught in his throat. The haunting melody transported him back to a time he'd rather forget - foxholes filled with mud and blood, the acrid smell of gunpowder hanging in the air, and the constant, gnawing fear of death. He closed his eyes, allowing the music to wash over him, a bittersweet reminder of the man he once was and the life he'd left behind.

A sharp, insistent knock at the door shattered the moment. Andrei's eyes snapped open, his hand instinctively reaching for a weapon that wasn't there. He forced himself to breathe, to slip back into the skin of Andrei Novikov, the unassuming Polish coach.

"One moment," he called out, his accent perfect as he moved towards the door. He opened it to find two men standing in the dimly lit hallway, their expressions hard and unyielding. The taller one, with close-cropped hair and a scar running along his jaw, spoke first.

"Andrei Novikov?" he asked, his voice clipped and authoritative.

Andrei nodded, feigning confusion. *"Yes, that's me. How can I help you?"*

The man flashed a KGB badge, *" I'm Agent Dimitry, we are your Russian welcoming committee."*

Without waiting for a response, the two men pushed past Andrei into the apartment. The space suddenly felt claustrophobic, the air thick with tension. Andrei's mind raced, calculating possible escape routes and weighing the odds of overpowering the agents. He dismissed the idea as quickly as it came - violence would only confirm their suspicions.

"Please, make yourselves comfortable," Andrei said, gesturing to the worn sofa. Neither man moved.

Dimitry's eyes darted around the room, taking in every detail. *"You've only recently arrived in Kirov, correct? Tell us about your background, Mr. Novikov. Why are you here?"*

Andrei launched into his prepared story, his words measured and calm despite the adrenaline coursing through his veins. *"I'm a coach, specializing in hockey. I was invited to observe the local teams. As for my background, I was born in Poland, but I've spent much of my life traveling, working with various teams across Eastern Europe."*

As he spoke, Dimitry's partner moved methodically through the apartment, opening drawers and examining

Andrei's meager possessions. Andrei fought to keep his expression neutral, knowing that any sign of distress could be fatal.

Suddenly, the partner paused near the radio, his head tilting slightly as he listened to the music still playing softly in the background. *"This song,"* he said, his voice surprisingly soft. *"It's 'Lubimiy Gorod', isn't it?"*

Andrei nodded, seizing the opportunity. *"Yes, it is. Do you know it?"*

The agent's stern facade cracked, just for a moment. *"My grandfather used to sing it. He fought in the war."*

Dimitry shot his partner a warning glance, but Andrei pressed on. *"The war,"* he said, his voice taking on a distant quality. *"I remember hearing this song then, too. In the trenches, when the nights were long and cold, and hope seemed so far away."*

The agents exchanged a look, their expressions softening almost imperceptibly. Andrei continued, weaving truth and fiction into a tapestry of shared experience. He spoke of the brutal cold, the constant fear, the camaraderie that bloomed even in the darkest moments. With each word, he saw the younger men lean in slightly, their eyes widening as they glimpsed a history they were too young to have lived.

"It was during a particularly harsh winter," Andrei said, his voice low and intense. *"We'd been pinned down for days, supplies running low. One night, as the temperature dropped to impossible lows, we heard it - 'Lubimiy Gorod', drifting across no man's land. For a moment, just a moment, the fighting stopped. We were all just men then, united by a song of home."*

Silence fell over the room as Andrei's words hung in the air. The agents stood still, caught between suspicion and a grudging respect for a veteran of a war they'd only heard about in stories.

Sensing the shift in atmosphere, Andrei made a decision. He moved slowly, telegraphing his movements as he walked to a small cupboard. *"Gentlemen,"* he said, pulling out a bottle of Moskovskaya vodka, *"perhaps we could continue this conversation over a drink? It's a fine Russian tradition, after all."*

Dimitry hesitated, his training warring with the unexpected turn the evening had taken. Finally, he gave a curt nod. *"One drink,"* he said, his tone still guarded but lacking its earlier hostility.

Andrei poured three glasses, his mind racing. The vodka was a gamble, but one that could pay off if played correctly. As he handed the glasses to the agents, he allowed himself a small, inward smile. The night was far from over, but for now, he had bought himself some time - and in the world of espionage, time could mean the difference between life and death.

The sharp scent of vodka cut through the lingering tension as Andrei poured three generous measures. The clear liquid caught the dim light, seeming to glow in the worn glasses. Dimitry, his stern facade cracking slightly, raised his glass first.

"To new acquaintances," he said, his voice gruff but lacking its earlier hostility.

Andrei nodded, lifting his own glass. *"And to the heroes of the past,"* he added, his eyes meeting those of Dimitry's partner.

As they drank, Dimitry's lips twitched in what might have been the ghost of a smile. "You know," he said, lowering his glass, *"I was named after Dmitri Mendeleev. The chemist."*

Andrei's eyebrows rose in genuine surprise. *"The creator of the periodic table? That's quite a legacy to live up to."*

Dimitry shrugged, but there was a hint of pride in his eyes. *"My father was a scientist. He believed in the power of knowledge."*

Sensing an opening, Andrei steered the conversation towards local matters. *"Speaking of knowledge, I'm still learning my way around Kirov. The ice rink, for instance - I've heard it's quite impressive."*

The younger agent, more relaxed now, nodded eagerly. *"Oh yes, it's state-of-the-art. They've been doing a lot of work there lately, upgrading equipment and such."*

Dimitry shot his partner a warning glance, but the damage was done. Andrei filed away the information, his mind racing with the implications. *"Upgrades? That's wonderful news for the team. Have there been many changes in town recently?"*

As the vodka flowed, so did the conversation. The agents, their guards lowered by alcohol and shared stories, let slip small details about recent activities in Kirov. Andrei listened intently, piecing together a mental map of the town's hidden landscape.

The bottle emptied far too quickly for Andrei's liking. As Dimitry and his partner rose to leave, their movements were less crisp, their expressions less guarded. *"Thank you for your hospitality, Mr. Novikov,"* Dimitry said, his words slightly slurred. *"Perhaps we misjudged you."*

Andrei inclined his head. *"It was my pleasure, gentlemen. I hope we'll meet again under more... relaxed circumstances."*

The door closed behind them with a soft click, and Andrei waited, counting his heartbeats until he was sure they were gone. Then, moving with a swiftness that belied his earlier show of inebriation, he began a thorough sweep of the apartment.

His fingers probed every crack, every crevice, his eyes scanning for anything out of place. Behind a loose baseboard near the radio, his hand brushed against something small and metallic. Andrei's breath caught in his throat as he carefully extracted a tiny listening device, no larger than a button.

"Clever bastards," he muttered, turning the bug over in his palm. Andrei spends several tense minutes contemplating his next move. Should he destroy the bug? Leave it in place and feed false information? As he weighed his options, a soft sound at the door catches his attention.

Cautiously, Andrei approaches the door. There, on the floor just inside, is a folded piece of paper that wasn't there before. He picks it up, his mind racing. This couldn't be from the KGB agents who just left - they wouldn't need to slip a message under the door. It must be from someone else, perhaps a local contact or even one of the missing agents he's here to find.

With trembling fingers, Andrei unfolds the paper. A series of numbers stares back at him. It takes him a moment to decipher the code, but when he does, his blood runs cold. The coordinates point to a location near the ice rink - a place he had mentally marked as a potential drop site just days ago.

Andrei sinks into a chair, the weight of the situation pressing down on him. This message complicates everything. Someone knows he's here, knows enough about his mission to direct him to a specific location. But who? And can they be trusted?

As the night wears on, Andrei finds his thoughts drifting to the baker he met earlier. He recalls her kind smile, the strength in her hands as she kneaded dough. For a moment, he allows himself to imagine a simpler life, one where he could pursue a relationship without the constant specter of danger.

But reality crashes back in. Andrei knows he can't afford such distractions. His mission is too important, the stakes too high. And yet, as he turns his focus back to the coded message and the bug, he can't quite shake the image of that beautiful lady from his mind.

Dawn breaks over Kirov, finding Andrei still awake, still grappling with his next move. The bug sits on the table, a silent reminder of the KGB's watchful eyes. The coded message lies beside it, an enigma from an unknown ally or enemy. And through it all, that beautiful face lingers in the back of his mind, a complication he never anticipated.

As the first rays of sunlight filter through his window, Andrei knows one thing for certain: the game has changed. His next moves will need to be even more careful, more calculated. With both the KGB and this mysterious message-sender watching his every move, the margin for error has shrunk to nothing. And somewhere in this dangerous equation, the bakery girl waits, an unknown variable that could tip the balance in ways Andrei can't yet foresee.

Chapter 7:
Cold Allies

The morning sun struggled to penetrate the thick Soviet smog as Andrei Novikov trudged through the streets of Kirov. His mind raced, replaying the events of the previous night - the KGB visit, the hidden bug, the cryptic message. Yet, despite the weight of his mission, his feet seemed to have a mind of their own, leading him back to the small bakery where he had first glimpsed her.

The aroma of fresh bread assaulted his senses as Andrei pushed open the door, the little bell above tinkling cheerfully. His eyes, trained to notice every detail, scanned the interior. Shelves lined with golden loaves, display cases filled with pastries, but no sign of her. Andrei's heart sank, though he chided himself for the reaction. He was here on a mission, not to chase after some baker he'd barely met.

Just as he was about to turn and leave, a flash of movement caught his eye. There, behind the counter, a figure ducked out of sight. Andrei's pulse quickened. He approached the counter, leaning over slightly to peer into the back room. Again, a flicker of movement, the swish of a skirt disappearing around a corner.

"Excuse me," Andrei called out, his voice steady despite the odd mix of frustration and excitement bubbling in his chest. "I was hoping to speak with one of your bakers."

A young man appeared from the back room, flour dusting his apron. "Which baker, sir?" he asked, his eyebrow raised in amusement.

Andrei hesitated. He didn't even know her name. "The woman," he said, feeling foolish. "Dark hair, about this tall." He gestured vaguely.

The young man's grin widened. "Ah, you must mean Taisiya. She's quite popular with our customers."

"Taisiya," Andrei repeated, the name rolling off his tongue. It felt right somehow. "Yes, I'd like to speak with her if possible."

The man's eyes twinkled with mischief. "Taisiya!" he called out. "You have an admirer!"

For a moment, nothing happened. Then, slowly, almost reluctantly, a figure emerged from the back room. Taisiya stood before him, her cheeks flushed, whether from the heat of the ovens or embarrassment, Andrei couldn't tell. Their eyes met, and the world seemed to narrow to just the two of them.

"Hello," Andrei said, his voice softer than he intended. "I'm Andrei. We met briefly the other day."

Taisiya nodded, a small smile playing at the corners of her mouth. "I remember. The newcomer to Kirov. How are you finding our city?"

"It's... interesting," Andrei replied, choosing his words carefully. "Though I must admit, I find myself drawn back to this bakery more often than I expected."

Taisiya's smile widened slightly, a flash of something - interest? amusement? - in her eyes. "Is it the bread that keeps bringing you back, Andrei?"

Andrei felt a warmth creeping up his neck. This wasn't how it was supposed to go. He was trained to maintain control, to never let his guard down. Yet here he was, flustered by a baker in a small Soviet town.

"Perhaps," he said, forcing a casual tone. "Though I find the company equally enticing." The words were out before he could stop them. Andrei cursed inwardly. What was he doing?

Taisiya's eyebrows rose, but before she could respond, Andrei blurted out, "Would you like to get coffee? After your shift, I mean. If you're free."

The bakery fell silent. Even the young man behind the counter seemed to be holding his breath. Taisiya studied Andrei for a long moment, her expression unreadable. Finally, she nodded. "Alright. I finish at four. Meet me here."

The hours crawled by as Andrei waited, alternating between berating himself for his recklessness and strategizing how to use this opportunity to gather information. When four o'clock finally arrived, he found himself back at the bakery, his palms uncharacteristically sweaty.

Taisiya emerged, her work clothes replaced by a simple dress, her hair loose around her shoulders. They walked in silence to a nearby café, the tension between them almost palpable.

As they settled at a small table, steaming cups of coffee before them, Andrei searched for something to say. "So, Taisiya," he began, wincing at how formal he sounded. "How long have you worked at the bakery?"

"Five years," she replied, her fingers tracing the rim of her cup. "It's not exciting work, but it's steady. In times like these, that's something to be grateful for."

Andrei nodded, noting the hint of resignation in her voice. "And before that?"

Taisiya's eyes flickered up to meet his. "Why so curious about my past, Andrei? Or should I be asking about yours?"

Andrei felt his muscles tense. Had he been too obvious? "I'm just trying to get to know you," he said, forcing a smile. "Isn't that what people do over coffee?"

Taisiya laughed; the sound unexpectedly warm in the austere café. "Fair enough. But let's make it a game. For every question I answer, you have to answer one too. Deal?"

Andrei hesitated. It was risky, but he needed to build trust. "Deal," he said, raising his cup in a mock toast.

What followed was a dance of words, each of them revealing small truths while guarding larger secrets. Andrei learned that Taisiya had grown up in a small village outside Kirov, that she had a brother who worked in a factory in Moscow, that she loved to read but found books increasingly hard to come by.

In return, he shared carefully crafted half-truths about his life in Poland, his love for hockey, his dreams of coaching a great team. With each exchange, he felt the wall between them lowering, just a fraction.

As their cups emptied and the afternoon light began to fade, Taisiya leaned back in her chair, a small smile playing on her lips. "This was... nice, Andrei. Unexpected, but nice."

Andrei nodded, surprised to find he agreed. Despite the constant vigilance required by his mission, he had enjoyed himself. It was a dangerous realization.

As they stood to leave, Taisiya turned to him. "The Vyatka Paleontological Museum is having a new exhibit opening this weekend. Would you like to go? It might help you get to know Kirov better."

Andrei's mind raced. The museum could be a goldmine of information about the city's history and layout. Plus, more time with Taisiya meant more opportunities to gather intelligence. And if a small part of him was simply looking forward to seeing her again, well, he could ignore that.

"I'd like that," he said, surprised by the genuine smile that spread across his face. "It's a date."

As they parted ways, Andrei felt a mix of excitement and dread settle in his stomach. He was making progress, but at what cost? In the game of espionage, personal connections were liabilities. Yet as he watched Taisiya disappear into the gathering dusk, he couldn't bring himself to regret the afternoon.

The real test, he knew, would come in the days ahead. Could he balance his mission with this budding... whatever it was? Only time would tell. For now, he had a museum date to prepare for, and a web of lies to maintain.

The days leading up to their museum visit passed in a blur of anticipation and careful planning. Andrei found himself torn between his meticulous mission preparations and an unexpected eagerness to see Taisiya again. As they walked together through Kirov's gray streets towards the museum,

Andrei's trained eyes constantly scanned for potential threats. Yet, he couldn't help but notice the way Taisiya's face lit up as she pointed out local landmarks, her enthusiasm a stark contrast to the drab surroundings. It was a dangerous distraction, he knew, but one he found increasingly difficult to resist as they approached the imposing structure of the Vyatka Paleontological Museum.

The Vyatka Paleontological Museum loomed before Andrei and Taisiya, its austere facade a stark contrast to the prehistoric wonders it housed within. Andrei's eyes darted across the building's exterior, cataloging potential exits and vantage points out of habit. Beside him, Taisiya's excitement was palpable, her eyes bright with anticipation.

"Shall we?" Andrei gestured towards the entrance, his voice steady despite the conflicting emotions churning inside him. This was an opportunity to gather crucial information, yet he couldn't ignore the warmth that spread through his chest at Taisiya's smile.

They entered the museum, the musty smell of age and preservation enveloping them. Andrei's trained senses went into overdrive, taking in every detail of their surroundings. The layout of the rooms, the positioning of the guards, the thickness of the walls - all potential intelligence filed away for later use.

As they moved through the exhibits, Andrei steered their conversation with practiced ease. "This building must have quite a history," he remarked, pausing before a display of fossilized mammoth bones. "Has it always been a museum?"

Taisiya shook her head, her hand brushing against Andrei's as she leaned in to examine the exhibit. The brief contact sent a jolt through him, a dangerous distraction he couldn't afford. "No, it was originally a merchant's mansion," she explained. "It was converted after the revolution. There have been rumors of renovations lately, though."

Andrei's ears perked up. "Renovations? What kind?"

"Oh, just whispers really. New security systems, restricted areas. Probably nothing." Taisiya shrugged, but Andrei noted the slight tension in her shoulders. There was more to this story, he was certain.

They continued through the museum, Andrei peppering their conversation with carefully crafted questions about Kirov's recent changes. Taisiya's answers, while seemingly innocuous, painted a picture of a city on edge, bracing for something big.

As they reached the final exhibit, a magnificently preserved cave bear skeleton, Andrei felt a surge of genuine excitement. His scientific curiosity, long buried under layers of espionage training, bubbled to the surface. "Would you look at that!" he exclaimed, forgetting himself for a moment. "Thank you for bringing me here, this is incredible!"

The words hung in the air, Andrei's crisp American accent echoing off the museum walls. He froze, the full weight of his mistake crashing down upon him. Beside him, Taisiya had gone rigid, her eyes wide with shock and... was that fear?

"Andrei?" Her voice was barely above a whisper, laced with confusion and growing suspicion. "Your accent..."

Andrei's mind raced, searching for a plausible explanation. But the damage was done. He could see the realization dawning in Taisiya's eyes, pieces of a puzzle she hadn't known she was solving falling into place.

With a quick glance around the room, Andrei gently but firmly grasped Taisiya's elbow, guiding her towards a secluded corner behind a large display case. "Taisiya, I can explain," he began, his voice low and urgent.

But Taisiya was already pulling away, her eyes flashing with a mixture of anger and betrayal. "Explain what, Andrei? Or is that even your real name?" Her words were sharp, cutting through the pretense they'd built over the past few days.

Andrei raised his hands in a placating gesture, acutely aware of how quickly the situation could spiral out of control. "Please, keep your voice down," he pleaded, his eyes darting around for any sign of unwanted attention. "You're right, there's more to me than I've let on. But this isn't the place to discuss it."

Taisiya's laugh was bitter, devoid of the warmth that had drawn Andrei to her. "Discuss it? You've been lying to me, to everyone. Who are you really? KGB? American spy?" Her voice dropped to a harsh whisper on the last word, the accusation hanging between them like a physical barrier.

Andrei felt the walls closing in. His training screamed at him to deny everything, to maintain his cover at all costs. But as he looked into Taisiya's eyes, seeing the hurt and confusion swirling there, he made a split-second decision that could very well cost him his life.

"Yes," he said simply, the admission heavy on his tongue. "I'm an American agent."

Taisiya's sharp intake of breath was the only sound in their secluded corner. For a long moment, neither of them moved, the weight of Andrei's confession pressing down on them both.

"Why?" Taisiya finally asked, her voice trembling slightly. "Why are you here? Why me?"

Andrei sighed; the burden of his secrets suddenly overwhelming. "I'm here to investigate something happening at the ice rink. Missing agents, possible weapons development. You... you weren't part of the plan. I never meant to involve you."

He watched Taisiya carefully, prepared for any reaction - screaming, running, perhaps even an attempt to alert the authorities. What he wasn't prepared for was the look of fierce determination that suddenly blazed in her eyes.

"Take me with you," she said, her voice low and intense.

Andrei blinked, certain he had misheard. "What?"

"When you leave, when your mission is over. Take me with you." Taisiya's words tumbled out in a rush, as if she feared losing her courage. "I've dreamed of escaping this place, of seeing the world beyond these walls. You're my chance."

Andrei's mind reeled. This was beyond anything he had anticipated. "Taisiya, you don't know what you're asking. It's dangerous, it's-"

"I know exactly what I'm asking," she cut him off, her eyes never leaving his. "I can help you. I know this city, its people, its secrets. You need me, Andrei, or whatever your real name is."

The offer hung between them, tempting and terrifying in equal measure. Andrei knew he should refuse, that involving a civilian in his mission was against every protocol he'd ever learned. But as he looked at Taisiya, saw the mixture of fear and hope in her eyes, he felt something shift inside him.

"John," he said quietly. "My real name is John."

Taisiya nodded, a small smile tugging at the corners of her mouth. "Nice to meet you, John. Now, shall we find somewhere more private to discuss our partnership?"

As they left the museum, walking close but not touching, Andrei felt as if he had stepped off a precipice. The ground beneath his feet was uncertain, the path ahead fraught with danger. But for the first time since arriving in Kirov, he felt a glimmer of hope. Whether it would be his salvation or his downfall remained to be seen.

The streets of Kirov seemed different now, charged with a new energy as Andrei and Taisiya made their way to a small, nondescript café. Every shadow held potential threats, every passerby a possible informant. Andrei's senses were on high alert, his body tense and ready for action.

As they settled into a corner booth, the weight of their new alliance hung heavy in the air. Andrei leaned in, his voice barely above a whisper. "Are you absolutely sure about this, Taisiya? Once we start down this path, there's no turning back."

Taisiya's eyes met his, unwavering. "I've been waiting for an opportunity like this my entire life, John. I'm ready."

And so, in hushed tones over lukewarm coffee, a most unlikely partnership was forged. As the sun set over Kirov, casting long shadows across the city, neither Andrei nor Taisiya could have imagined the dangerous path that lay ahead of them, or the profound impact their alliance would have on the cold war chessboard.

The days following their museum confrontation blurred into a whirlwind of clandestine meetings and hushed conversations. Andrei and Taisiya met in shadowy corners of forgotten cafes, their heads bent close together over steaming cups of bitter coffee. Each encounter was a delicate dance of trust and suspicion, information traded like precious currency.

"The KGB has been more active lately," Taisiya murmured, her eyes darting to the cafe's entrance. "There's talk of increased patrols around the ice rink. People are nervous."

Andrei nodded, filing away the information. "Any idea why?"

Taisiya's lips tightened. "Rumors of American spies. They're paranoid, seeing threats in every shadow."

The irony wasn't lost on Andrei. He leaned back, his mind racing. "What else?"

As Taisiya spoke, painting a picture of Kirov's underground currents, Andrei felt a growing sense of unease. The KGB's net was tightening, and he was running out of time.

The opportunity came unexpectedly. A flyer, tacked to a bulletin board outside the local sports complex, caught

Andrei's eye. The Kirov hockey team was holding open tryouts for a new assistant coach. It was a risk, but one he had to take.

The day of the tryout dawned cold and gray. Andrei stood at the edge of the ice rink, his breath misting in the chilly air. Around him, other hopefuls stretched and murmured, their eyes filled with a mixture of hope and resignation.

As Andrei stepped onto the ice, muscle memory took over. He demonstrated drills, barked orders, his voice carrying with the authority of years of experience. The head coach, a grizzled man with hard eyes, watched impassively.

When it was over, Andrei stood before the coach, heart pounding beneath his calm exterior. The coach's words were gruff, tinged with reluctant admiration. "You've got skills, Novikov. But we don't know you. Best I can offer is equipment manager, for now. Prove yourself, maybe you'll move up."

It wasn't ideal, but it was a foot in the door. Andrei accepted with a nod, careful not to let his excitement show.

That evening, as he made his way to meet Taisiya, the weight of his new position pressed upon him. He should tell her, he knew. It was vital information, a significant step in his mission. But as he rounded the corner and saw her waiting, a nagging doubt held him back. How much could he truly trust her?

The decision was made for him as a shout rang out behind them. "Stop! Identity check!"

Andrei's blood ran cold. He grabbed Taisiya's arm, pulling her into a narrow alley. They pressed themselves against the damp brick wall, hearts pounding in unison as heavy footsteps approached.

The moment stretched, taut with tension. Andrei could feel Taisiya's rapid breath against his neck, the warmth of her body a stark contrast to the cold fear gripping his chest. The footsteps paused at the alley's entrance. Andrei's hand tightened on Taisiya's arm, ready to run or fight.

An eternity passed in seconds. Then, mercifully, the footsteps moved on. Andrei and Taisiya remained frozen, neither daring to move until the sound had faded completely.

Finally, Taisiya turned to him, her eyes wide in the darkness. "That was close," she whispered, her voice trembling slightly.

Andrei nodded, suddenly acutely aware of their proximity. In that moment, as the adrenaline coursed through his veins and Taisiya's warmth seeped into him, he felt the weight of his secret press against his chest. The news of his position at the ice rink burned on the tip of his tongue, urging to be shared. But caution held him back.

"We should be more careful," he murmured instead, his eyes scanning the alley's entrance. "They're getting bolder."

Taisiya nodded, her gaze never leaving his face. "We're in this together now," she said softly, a hint of steel in her voice.

As they stood there, hearts still racing, bodies close in the narrow alley, Andrei felt something shift. The last vestiges of doubt about their alliance melted away, replaced by a certainty that, for better or worse, their fates were now irrevocably intertwined. Yet, the secret of his new position remained his alone, a reminder of the delicate balance between trust and caution in the world of espionage.

Chapter 8:
Unseen Eyes

The cold Kirov night enveloped Andrei as he made his way back to his apartment, the echoes of his and Taisiya's rapid heartbeats still pulsing in his ears. The narrow escape from the KGB patrol had left him shaken, more alert than ever to the dangers that lurked in every shadow. As he climbed the creaking stairs to his floor, Andrei's mind raced, replaying every moment of his interaction with Taisiya in the alley.

Their alliance was deepening, that much was clear. The way she had pressed against him in the darkness, the trust in her eyes as they faced danger together - it all spoke of a connection that went beyond mere cooperation. Yet, as Andrei unlocked his door and stepped into the spartan safety of his apartment, the weight of his secrets pressed down on him. The position at the ice rink burned in his chest, demanding to be shared. But years of training held his tongue. In this game, trust was a luxury he couldn't afford, not yet.

Andrei collapsed onto his bed, fully clothed, his eyes fixed on the cracked ceiling. Sleep eluded him as his mind churned with possibilities and dangers. The ice rink position was a crucial breakthrough, but it also placed him squarely in the KGB's crosshairs. One wrong move, one misplaced word, and everything could come crashing down.

As dawn broke over Kirov, painting the sky in muted grays and pinks, Andrei made a decision. He needed to see Taisiya, to gauge her loyalty, to ensure their alliance was as strong as he hoped. With renewed purpose, he set out for the bakery, his senses on high alert for any sign of surveillance.

The familiar scent of fresh bread enveloped Andrei as he pushed open the bakery door, the little bell tinkling overhead. Taisiya looked up from behind the counter, surprise and something warmer flashing in her eyes. "Jo- Andrei," she caught herself, glancing quickly around the empty shop. "I wasn't expecting you."

Andrei approached the counter, his voice low. "I needed to see you. To talk."

Understanding dawned on Taisiya's face. She nodded, reaching for a loaf of bread. As she wrapped it, Andrei noticed her fingers moving with deliberate care, pressing something into the paper. "Here," she said, her voice steady but her eyes conveying volumes. "Try this one. It's a new recipe."

As Andrei reached for the loaf, a sharp knock at the door made them both freeze. Through the glass, the unmistakable silhouette of a KGB officer loomed. Taisiya's eyes widened in panic, but Andrei's mind was already racing.

In one fluid motion, he grabbed a knife from the counter, slicing into the bread even, while she called out, "Come in!" His fingers found the edge of Taisiya's note, deftly separating it from the wrapper as he cut the loaf. With practiced ease, he slid the paper between two slices, his movements hidden by the counter.

The KGB agent strode in, his cold eyes sweeping the bakery before settling on Andrei. "Andrei Novikov," he stated, more an accusation than a greeting. "What a surprise to find you here so early."

Andrei straightened, his face a mask of polite confusion. "Good morning, officer. Is there a problem?" He extended his hand in greeting, a gesture both courteous and calculated. The officer grasped it, attempting to establish dominance with an iron grip. But years of kneading dough had given Andrei's hands a strength that surprised the KGB man. Their eyes met, a silent battle of wills, until the officer's grip slackened first, a flicker of uncertainty crossing his face.

The agent's lips twitched in what might have been a smirk, though it lacked his earlier confidence. "No problem. Just a routine check. We like to keep an eye on new arrivals to our city." His gaze shifted to the bread in Andrei's hands. "Doing some shopping, I see."

"Ah, yes," Andrei replied, forcing a light chuckle. "I've become quite fond of the bread here. Taisiya was just telling me about this new recipe they're trying."

The agent's eyes narrowed, flicking between Andrei and Taisiya. "Is that so? You two seem... friendly."

Taisiya stepped forward, her voice steady despite the tension Andrei could see in her shoulders. "I try to be friendly with all our customers, officer. It's good for business."

The agent hummed noncommittally, his hand resting casually on his holstered pistol. "And how long have you known our friend Andrei here?"

"Only since he arrived in Kirov," Taisiya answered smoothly. "He's become a regular customer."

Andrei nodded, taking a bite of the bread to cover any tells that might betray him. "It's delicious," he said, careful to maintain eye contact with the agent. "You should try some yourself, officer. A taste of Kirov's finest."

For a long moment, the agent said nothing, his gaze boring into Andrei as if trying to peel back layers of deception. Finally, he shrugged. "Perhaps another time. Enjoy your bread, Comrade Novikov. And do remember, we're always watching. For your safety, of course."

With that thinly veiled threat hanging in the air, the agent turned and left, the bell's cheerful tinkle a stark contrast to the tension he left behind.

As soon as the door closed, Taisiya sagged against the counter, her breath coming in short gasps. "That was too close," she whispered.

Andrei nodded, his own heart racing despite his outward calm. "We need to be more careful," he murmured, his eyes still fixed on the door. "They're watching us closer than we thought."

In the days that followed, Andrei felt the weight of unseen eyes on him constantly. Every time he left his apartment, he noticed the same nondescript car parked across the street. At the ice rink, new "maintenance workers" appeared, their eyes too sharp, their questions too pointed to be mere janitors.

Andrei adapted, drawing on years of training to evade detection. He varied his routes to work, used the crowded marketplace to lose potential tails, and developed a complex system of signals with Taisiya to arrange safe meetings. But the constant vigilance took its toll.

Each night, Andrei returned to his apartment exhausted, not just physically but mentally. The strain of maintaining his cover, of watching every word and gesture, wore on him. He found himself jumping at shadows, second-guessing every interaction.

Yet even as the pressure mounted, Andrei couldn't shake the feeling that he was close to a breakthrough. The increased KGB presence had to mean something. Whatever was happening at the ice rink, whatever had happened to the missing agents, it was big enough to warrant this level of scrutiny.

As Andrei lay in bed, staring at the ceiling and listening for any unusual sounds outside his door, he knew one thing with certainty: the game was escalating. The stakes were higher than ever, and one wrong move could spell disaster not just for him, but for Taisiya as well. With that sobering thought, he closed his eyes, steeling himself for whatever challenges the next day might bring.

The morning came too soon, the weak sunlight filtering through his threadbare curtains doing little to dispel the shadows of the night. Andrei rose, his body protesting after another restless night, and prepared for his shift at the ice rink. As he dressed, his mind churned with plans and contingencies, each step of his morning routine accompanied by a mental checklist of potential threats and escape routes. The weight of his mission pressed down on him, a constant reminder of the delicate balance he walked between success and catastrophe.

Arriving at the rink, Andrei slipped into his role as the unassuming equipment manager, the harsh fluorescent lights glaring down on him as he meticulously polished the blade of a skate. His muscles ached from the day's exertions, but his mind remained sharp, constantly alert for any signs of danger or opportunity.

"Novikov!" The gruff voice of Coach Volkov echoed across the empty rink. "A word."

Andrei set down the skate, his heart rate quickening despite his outward calm. He approached the coach, noting the man's furrowed brow and the way his eyes darted around the rink, as if checking for eavesdroppers.

"Your suggestion about changing our defensive strategy," Volkov began, his voice low. "It worked. The team's performance has improved significantly."

Andrei nodded, careful to keep his expression neutral. "I'm glad I could help, Coach."

Volkov's eyes narrowed, studying Andrei with newfound interest. "Where did you say you trained again?"

"Various places across Eastern Europe," Andrei replied smoothly, the lie practiced and polished. "I've picked up different techniques over the years."

The coach grunted, seemingly satisfied. "Well, keep it up. The higher-ups are starting to take notice. Who knows? You might be moving up from equipment manager sooner than you think."

As Volkov walked away, Andrei allowed himself a small smile. His cover was solidifying, his position at the rink growing more secure. But with that progress came increased scrutiny, and the weight of constant vigilance pressed down on him like a physical force.

Later that night, in the suffocating darkness of his small apartment, Andrei lay wide awake, his eyes fixed on the ceiling. Every creak of the building, every distant shout from the street below, set his nerves on edge. Sleep, when it came, was fitful and plagued by nightmares of pursuit and capture.

He jolted awake at dawn, his shirt soaked with sweat, the echoes of imagined gunshots still ringing in his ears. As he splashed cold water on his face, Andrei barely recognized the haggard man staring back at him from the mirror. Dark circles shadowed his eyes, and a constant tick had developed in his left cheek.

The streets of Kirov seemed to pulse with hidden dangers as Andrei made his way to the rink. Every face he passed was a potential KGB agent, every parked car a possible surveillance post. He found himself taking increasingly complex routes, doubling back and using crowds as cover, all the while scanning for the telltale signs of a tail.

It was on one such circuitous journey that Andrei spotted him - a man in a nondescript gray coat, moving with too much purpose to be a casual pedestrian. Their eyes met for a split second across the crowded street, and Andrei's blood ran cold. He'd been made.

Without breaking stride, Andrei ducked into a narrow alley, his mind racing. The twisting backstreets Taisiya had described to him flashed through his memory. He took a sharp left, then a right, weaving through the labyrinthine heart of old Kirov.

The sound of rapid footsteps behind him spurred Andrei on. He vaulted over a low wall, landing in a trash-strewn courtyard. A startled cat yowled and darted away as he sprinted across the open space, his lungs burning.

Andrei burst out onto a busier street, immediately blending into the flow of morning commuters. He risked a glance back, his heart pounding. The gray-coated man was nowhere to be seen, but Andrei knew better than to relax. He maintained his brisk pace, taking a deliberately confusing route until he finally arrived at the ice rink, shaken but uncompromised.

The close call left Andrei even more on edge. He threw himself into his work at the rink, scrubbing floors and sharpening skates with a manic intensity that drew curious glances from the other staff. But beneath the facade of the diligent worker, Andrei's senses remained on high alert, constantly scanning for any hint of danger.

It was during one of these late-night cleaning sessions, as Andrei methodically mopped the locker room floor, that he heard it - hushed voices drifting from the coach's office. He froze, straining to listen.

"The project is proceeding as planned," a low voice murmured. "The modifications to the facility are nearly complete."

"And the test?" a second voice asked, tense with anticipation.

"Soon. We've received coordinates for the site. It's remote, well away from prying eyes."

Andrei's breath caught in his throat. Coordinates. The cryptic message he'd received weeks ago flashed through his mind. Could this be connected?

"And what of our... guests?" the second voice inquired delicately.

A dark chuckle. "They've been most cooperative, now that they understand the consequences of refusal. Their expertise has been invaluable."

The conversation moved on to mundane matters, but Andrei had heard enough. He finished his cleaning with mechanical precision, his mind racing to process the implications of what he'd overheard.

Back in the relative safety of his apartment, Andrei pored over the coded message he'd received, cross-referencing it with maps of the surrounding area. As the pieces fell into place, a chill ran down his spine. The coordinates matched a remote area deep in the nearby forests - the perfect location for a clandestine weapons test.

And the "guests" - the biggest question was who were they? Andrei's hands shook as he scribbled down his findings. The stakes had just risen exponentially. This wasn't just about missing agents anymore; it was about preventing a potentially catastrophic weapons test. And he was the only one who could stop it.

As the first light of dawn crept through his grimy window, Andrei made a decision. He needed to act, and soon. But he couldn't do it alone. Despite the risk, despite his reservations, he knew he had to bring Taisiya fully into his confidence. Her knowledge of the area, her connections in the city - they would be crucial in the days to come.

Andrei tucked his notes into a hidden compartment in the sole of his shoe, his jaw set with grim determination. The game had changed, the consequences of failure now too terrible to contemplate. As he prepared to face another day under the watchful eyes of the KGB, Andrei knew that the real test of his skills - and his courage - was only just beginning.

Chapter 9: Confrontation

A group of Young Pioneers marched past, their red scarves bright against the gray Kirov evening, as Andrei wove through the city's winding streets. His mind raced with the revelations from the ice rink. The weight of his discovery – a secret weapons test, missing agents forced to cooperate – pressed down on him like a physical force. Every shadow seemed to conceal a potential threat, every passerby a possible KGB operative.

Andrei's eyes darted from side to side, scanning for signs of surveillance. He'd taken a circuitous route from the rink, doubling back and weaving through crowded marketplaces in an attempt to shake any tail. But the nagging feeling of being watched persisted, prickling at the back of his neck.

As he rounded a corner onto a quieter street, Andrei's heart nearly stopped. There, not ten feet away, stood an imposing figure in a KGB uniform. The officer's steel-gray eyes locked onto Andrei's, a flash of suspicion igniting in their depths.

For a split second, time seemed to freeze. Andrei's mind whirled, calculating escape routes, assessing the threat. The officer's hand twitched towards his coat, where Andrei suspected a pistol was concealed.

"Comrade Novikov," the officer's voice cut through the tension, smooth as silk but with an undercurrent of steel. "What a fortunate encounter. I've been hoping to speak with you."

Andrei forced his features into a mask of casual surprise. "Officer...?" he replied, feigning ignorance of the man's identity while fighting to keep his voice steady.

"Orlov. Viktor Orlov," the officer supplied, his lips curling into a humorless smile. "Perhaps we could have a word? In private."

Before Andrei could protest, Orlov's hand clamped down on his shoulder, steering him into a narrow alley between two dilapidated buildings. The sounds of the street faded, replaced by the pounding of Andrei's own heart in his ears.

Orlov released his grip but positioned himself to block the alley's exit. His eyes never left Andrei's face, scrutinizing every micro-expression. "You've been quite... active lately, Comrade Novikov. For a simple equipment manager, your movements are remarkably complex."

Andrei's blood ran cold, but he maintained his composure. "I'm not sure what you mean, Officer Orlov," he replied, forcing a confused smile. "I've simply been adjusting to life in Kirov, as any new arrival would."

Orlov's eyebrow arched. "Indeed? And does 'adjusting' typically involve such frequent visits to a certain bakery? Or perhaps your late-night wanderings around the ice rink are part of your... acclimation process?"

The implicit threat in Orlov's words was clear. Andrei's mind raced, searching for a plausible explanation that wouldn't further incriminate him. "I've always been a night owl," he said with a forced chuckle. "And as for the bakery, well, a man has to eat, doesn't he?"

Orlov's eyes narrowed, his gaze boring into Andrei. "A man does indeed need to eat. But a man also needs to be careful about the company he keeps. Your friendship with the baker girl, for instance – it would be a shame if anything were to... happen to her."

Andrei's fists clenched at his sides, a surge of protective anger flaring in his chest. He fought to keep it from showing on his face. "The baker is simply an acquaintance," he said, his voice tight. "Nothing more."

"Is that so?" Orlov's tone was deceptively light, but his eyes glittered dangerously. "Then perhaps you won't mind explaining why you two have been seen having such... intense conversations? Or why you seem to take such circuitous routes to and from her bakery?"

Each word was like a dagger, revealing the extent of the KGB's surveillance. Andrei felt the noose tightening around him, his carefully constructed cover threatening to unravel.

As the tension in the alley reached a fever pitch, Andrei caught a glimpse of something in Orlov's eyes – a flicker of personal determination that went beyond mere duty. For a moment, he wondered what drove this man, what personal stakes fueled his relentless pursuit.

Suddenly, the world around them seemed to blur, the grimy walls of the alley fading away as the narrative shifted, offering a glimpse into Viktor Orlov's past.

A young Viktor stood at attention, his back ramrod straight as he faced a panel of stern-faced officers. The room was thick with cigarette smoke and unspoken accusations.

"Orlov," one of the officers barked, "your family's history is... problematic. How can we trust you to serve the State when your own father was accused of treason?"

Viktor's jaw clenched, but his voice remained steady. "My father was falsely accused, Comrade. I am here to restore honor to the Orlov name through loyal service to the Soviet Union."

The scene shifted, showing Viktor pouring over documents late into the night, his eyes red-rimmed but determined. Another flash: Viktor leading raids on suspected foreign agents, his face a mask of grim resolve. Then, Viktor standing over a map of Kirov, his finger tracing the outline of the ice rink with laser-like focus.

A final image materialized: Viktor alone in his office, staring at a dossier. The name "Andrei Novikov" was clearly visible on the cover. "There's something not right about you, Novikov," he murmured. "And I will uncover it. For the glory of the Soviet Union... and for my family's redemption."

The flashback ended as abruptly as it had begun, snapping back to the tense standoff in the alley. Andrei blinked, momentarily disoriented by the unexpected insight into Orlov's psyche. The KGB officer's eyes remained fixed on him, burning with an intensity that now carried new meaning.

Orlov leaned in closer, his voice low and menacing. "I hope you understand, Comrade Novikov, that nothing escapes our notice. Nothing."

The implications hung heavy in the air between them. Andrei knew he was walking a razor's edge, one misstep away from exposure and certain doom. But now, armed with this fleeting glimpse into Orlov's motivations, he felt a new dimension added to their dangerous game of cat and mouse.

Andrei's mind raced, acutely aware of the precipice he stood upon. Fleeing would confirm Orlov's suspicions, but staying put under this relentless interrogation risked exposing his true identity. He forced a calm he didn't feel, adopting a posture of mild confusion tinged with indignation.

"Officer Orlov," Andrei began, his voice steady despite the adrenaline coursing through his veins, "I appreciate your dedication to security, but I fear there's been a misunderstanding. My 'complex movements,' as you call them, are simply the result of my curiosity about Kirov. I'm new here, eager to explore."

Orlov's eyes narrowed; skepticism etched in the lines of his face. "And the bakery? Your frequent visits there?"

Andrei allowed a sheepish smile to cross his face. "Ah, well, I have a bit of a sweet tooth, I'm afraid. And the baker, Taisiya, she's been kind enough to help me practice my Russian. My accent still needs work, you see."

He watched Orlov carefully, noting the slight twitch in the KGB officer's jaw. The explanation was plausible, but Orlov wasn't entirely convinced. Andrei pressed on, seizing control of the narrative.

"As for my late nights at the rink, surely you're aware I've been put in charge of equipment maintenance? The team's performance has improved significantly since I've been ensuring the skates and sticks are in top condition. You can ask Coach Volkov himself."

Orlov opened his mouth to respond, but at that moment, a cacophony of shouts and the sound of shattering glass erupted from the street beyond the alley. Both men instinctively turned towards the commotion.

"Brawl at the tavern," Andrei observed, recognizing an opportunity. "Seems like it's getting out of hand. Shouldn't you...?"

Orlov hesitated, clearly torn between his duty to maintain order and his desire to continue the interrogation. Andrei seized the moment, subtly shifting the conversation.

"You know, Officer Orlov, I understand your suspicion. These are tense times, and you have a vital job to do. Perhaps we could continue this discussion in a more official capacity? I'd be happy to come to your office and answer any questions you might have. Transparently, of course."

The suggestion caught Orlov off guard. His eyes flickered between Andrei and the growing disturbance in the street. Finally, he nodded curtly.

"Very well, Novikov. Let's meet another time then. We'll have a more... thorough discussion then."

Andrei nodded, relief washing over him even as he maintained his facade of polite cooperation. "Of course, Officer. I'll be looking forward to it."

As Orlov strode out of the alley to deal with the brawl, Andrei let out a breath he hadn't realized he'd been holding. He'd bought himself some time, but the danger was far from over. With measured steps, he emerged from the alley and melted into the evening crowd, hyperaware of every glance cast his way.

Andrei returned unharmed to his apartment, Andrei's mind whirled with the implications of the encounter. Orlov was more than just a dedicated KGB officer; there was a personal stake driving his relentless pursuit. The glimpse into Orlov's past – the family's tarnished honor, the burning desire for redemption – added a new layer of complexity to an already perilous situation.

Andrei paced the worn floorboards, piecing together the puzzle. Orlov's family history made him dangerous in ways that went beyond mere ideology. A man with something to prove, with a personal vendetta against perceived enemies of the state, would stop at nothing to uncover the truth.

The weight of his mission pressed down on Andrei with renewed force. He wasn't just up against the KGB machine; he was facing a man whose entire sense of self was tied to rooting out threats to the Soviet Union. One wrong move, one slip in his cover, and Orlov would pounce with the full force of a man reclaiming his family's honor.

As the night deepened, Andrei's thoughts turned to Taisiya. His connection to her had not gone unnoticed, and now she was in danger by association. He would need to warn her, to prepare her for the increased scrutiny that was sure to come. But how much could he reveal without putting her at even greater risk?

The mission had become a deadly chess match, with Orlov as a formidable opponent. Andrei knew he would need every ounce of his training, every shred of his wit, to stay one step ahead.

Meanwhile, in his dimly lit office at KGB headquarters, Viktor Orlov sat hunched over his desk, a tumbler of vodka untouched at his elbow. His eyes, bloodshot from long hours and relentless focus, scanned the dossier spread before him. Andrei Novikov's file was frustratingly thin, the details of his background just a little too perfect, too neatly arranged.

Orlov's fingers drummed an agitated rhythm on the worn wood of his desk. The encounter in the alley played over in his mind, each word, each micro-expression of Novikov's face analyzed and reanalyzed. The man's explanations were plausible, maddeningly so. Yet something nagged at Orlov, a sense honed by years of rooting out enemies of the state.

He reached for a cigarette, the familiar ritual doing little to calm his racing thoughts. As he struck a match, the flame illuminated a framed photograph on his desk – a stern-faced man in military uniform, Orlov's father before the accusations of treason had torn their family apart.

Viktor's jaw clenched, a muscle twitching beneath the skin. He had sworn on his father's grave to restore the Orlov name, to prove through unwavering loyalty and service that their blood ran red with devotion to the Soviet cause. Every traitor uncovered, every threat neutralized, was a step towards redemption.

But Novikov... Orlov couldn't shake the feeling that he was missing something crucial. The man's behavior was just odd enough to raise flags, yet his responses under pressure had been smooth, almost too polished.

Orlov took a long drag on his cigarette, the smoke curling around him like the tendrils of doubt clouding his mind. He had pushed hard in the alley, perhaps too hard. If Novikov was truly an innocent equipment manager, such aggressive questioning might drive him to make a complaint. But if he was hiding something...

A knock at the door interrupted Orlov's brooding. "Enter," he barked, straightening in his chair.

A junior officer stepped in, saluting crisply. "Sir, the report on the tavern brawl."

Orlov waved a dismissive hand. "Leave it on the desk. Anything else?"

The young man hesitated. "Well, sir, there's a rumor going around. Some of the locals are saying they saw a man fitting Novikov's description talking to one of the known black market dealers last week."

Orlov's eyes narrowed, a predatory gleam igniting in their depths. "Is that so? Interesting. Very interesting indeed. Dismissed."

As the door closed behind the junior officer, a grim smile played at the corners of Orlov's mouth. Perhaps this was the thread that, when pulled, would unravel Novikov's carefully constructed facade. Tomorrow's interview promised to be very enlightening indeed.

Orlov crushed out his cigarette, his weariness forgotten in the face of this new lead. The hunt was on, and Viktor Orlov would not rest until he uncovered the truth – for the glory of the Soviet Union, and for the honor of the Orlov name.

Chapter 10: Unraveling Secrets

A group of factory workers shuffled past, their faces weary from long shifts, as Andrei made his way through Kirov's winding streets. The acrid smell of industrial smoke hung in the air, a constant reminder of the city's relentless push for progress. His mind still reeled from the encounter with Orlov. Every shadow seemed to conceal a potential threat, every passerby a possible KGB informant. The weight of his mission, coupled with the newfound knowledge of Orlov's personal vendetta, pressed down on him like a physical force.

Andrei's fingers brushed against the rough brick of a building as he ducked into a narrow alley, his eyes scanning for any sign of surveillance. Satisfied he wasn't being followed, he pulled out a crumpled piece of paper from his coat pocket. The hastily scrawled note from Taisiya confirmed their meeting at the Vyatka Paleontological Museum. It was a risk, but one he had to take. He needed information, and more than that, he needed a moment of respite from the constant tension that threatened to overwhelm him.

The museum loomed before him, its austere facade a stark contrast to the prehistoric wonders it housed within.

Andrei paused at the entrance, his trained eyes cataloging potential escape routes and vantage points. As he pushed open the heavy doors, the musty smell of age and preservation enveloped him.

Taisiya stood by a display of fossilized trilobites, her face lighting up with a smile that didn't quite reach her eyes. The strain of their dangerous alliance was evident in the tightness of her shoulders, the way her gaze darted nervously around the room.

"Fancy meeting you here, comrade," Andrei said, pitching his voice just loud enough to be overheard by the bored-looking museum attendant. "These old bones are fascinating, aren't they?"

Taisiya nodded, falling into step beside him as they moved deeper into the museum. "Indeed. It's amazing how much we can learn from the past," she replied, her words laden with double meaning.

They wandered through the exhibits, their conversation a carefully orchestrated dance of innocuous observations and coded messages. To any observer, they would appear as nothing more than two friends sharing an interest in paleontology. But beneath the surface, vital information was exchanged.

"The mammoth tusks are impressive," Taisiya murmured, leaning close to examine a display. "But I heard a rumor about a new exhibit coming soon. Something about recent discoveries in the permafrost."

Andrei's ears perked up. "Recent discoveries" could mean new developments in the case of the missing agents. "Oh? Where did you hear that?" he asked, his tone casual even as his heart raced.

"Oh, you know how people talk," Taisiya shrugged, her eyes meeting his for a brief, meaningful moment. "Especially after a few drinks at the tavern near the ice rink."

Andrei filed away the information, his mind already working to decipher the hidden message. The tavern near the ice rink was a known hangout for low-level KGB officers. If Taisiya had overheard something there, it could be crucial.

As they moved through the museum, Andrei's senses remained on high alert. Every creak of the floorboards, every murmur from other visitors, set his nerves on edge.

As Andrei and Taisiya exited the museum, the cold Kirov air nipped at their faces. They strolled casually along the building's exterior, their conversation deliberately mundane to avoid suspicion. Andrei's eyes, ever vigilant, scanned their surroundings out of habit.

Suddenly, a glint in the late afternoon sun caught his attention. Andrei's gaze dropped to a grimy basement window, half-obscured by a small drift of snow. His heart skipped a beat.

There, etched in the dust and grime, was an unmistakable symbol - the interlocking NY logo of the New York Yankees. Andrei's steps faltered for a split second before he forced himself to keep walking, his mind racing.

He couldn't stop. He couldn't stare. Any unusual behavior could draw unwanted attention. But that logo... Only an American would draw that, and not just any American - a New Yorker, a Yankees fan.

Andrei's pulse quickened. The missing operative from New York, flashed through his mind. This had to be a message, a sign that he was alive, that he had been here.

Keeping his voice steady, Andrei continued his conversation with Taisiya, fighting the urge to look back at the window. "The mammoth exhibit was quite impressive, wasn't it?" he said, his tone casual even as his fingers tapped out a subtle code on his thigh, alerting Taisiya to the discovery.

Taisiya's eyes widened almost imperceptibly as she caught the signal. Without missing a beat, she fumbled in her purse, producing a small compact mirror. Under the guise of checking her appearance, she angled the mirror to capture a reflection of the etched logo.

"Oh, darling, you have a smudge on your cheek," she said, her voice light but her eyes intense. She reached up, ostensibly to wipe Andrei's face, using the motion to obscure her other hand as she quickly sketched the logo on a scrap of paper hidden in her palm.

The moment stretched, fraught with tension, as they worked to document the discovery without arousing suspicion. Andrei's mind raced, calculating the odds that they were being watched, planning their next move.

As they finally walked away from the museum, the weight of their discovery hung heavy between them. They parted ways with a casual goodbye, but Andrei could see the barely contained excitement and fear in Taisiya's eyes. They both knew the stakes had just been raised significantly.

Later that night, secure within the walls of his apartment, Andrei sat at his rickety desk, a single lamp casting long shadows across the room. His hands, steady despite the adrenaline still coursing through his veins, carefully crafted a coded message to Arthur.

The code was complex, a series of seemingly innocuous phrases about hockey strategies and equipment maintenance. But hidden within were the crucial details of his discovery at the museum.

"New stick design shows promise. Resembles famous New York model. Advise on compatibility with our team."

Andrei read and reread the message, checking for any errors that could jeopardize the operation. Satisfied, he sealed the envelope, ready to be sent through one of their established dead drops.

As he stared at the sealed message, the full weight of his situation pressed down on him. The Yankees logo was a clear sign from the missing operative from New York. It was proof of life, but also a stark reminder of the danger they all faced.

Andrei leaned back in his chair, his eyes drifting to the window where the lights of Kirov flickered in the distance. Somewhere out there, the missing agents were being held. Somewhere, the KGB was pushing forward with their secret weapons program. And here he was, walking a tightrope between discovery and success, with the fate of not just the mission, but perhaps the entire Cold War hanging in the balance.

With a deep breath, Andrei stood, preparing to make the perilous journey to the dead drop location. As he donned his coat and hat, he allowed himself a grim smile. The game was afoot, and despite the danger, despite the odds stacked against him, Andrei felt a familiar thrill. This was what he was trained for, what he lived for. And come hell or high water, he would see this mission through to the end.

The cold Kirov night enveloped Andrei as he made his way to the small, dimly lit café where he was to meet Taisiya. His breath frosted in the air, a visible reminder of the constant chill that seemed to permeate every aspect of life in this Soviet outpost. As he pushed open the door, the warmth inside hit him like a wall, bringing with it the rich aroma of coffee and the low murmur of hushed conversations.

Taisiya sat in a corner booth; her fingers wrapped around a steaming cup. Her eyes, usually bright and alert, were shadowed with fatigue and worry. Andrei slid into the seat across from her, his back to the wall, giving him a clear view of the entire café.

"You look like you haven't slept," he murmured, his voice low.

Taisiya's lips twitched in a humorless smile. "Sleep is a luxury these days. But I've got something for you."

She leaned in, her voice dropping to barely above a whisper. "There's been talk at the market. Whispers about strange deliveries to an old warehouse on the outside of town. Heavy crates, armed guards. There’s something else - one of the dock workers swears he heard American voices."

Andrei's pulse quickened, but he kept his face impassive. "Interesting. Anything else?"

Taisiya nodded, her eyes darting around the café before continuing. "The night watchman from the ice rink - he's been there every night this week, drinking more than usual. Last night, he got pretty loose lipped. Started bragging about a big bonus he'd received. Said it was for 'keeping his eyes closed and his mouth shut' about some 'special visitors' to the facility after hours."

As Taisiya spoke, Andrei's mind raced, piecing together this new information with what he already knew. The Yankees logo at the museum, the intercepted conversations about a secret project, and now these rumors of American voices and clandestine meetings at the ice rink - it was all starting to form a cohesive picture.

The missing agents were alive, that much was clear. They were being held somewhere on the outskirts of Kirov, possibly in that warehouse Taisiya mentioned. And whatever the KGB was forcing them to work on, it was connected to the ice rink. But why? What could they possibly be developing that required both a remote warehouse and a busy sports facility?

Andrei's thoughts were interrupted by the scrape of Taisiya's chair as she stood to leave. "Be careful," she whispered, her hand briefly squeezing his shoulder. "The eyes are everywhere."

As Taisiya's figure disappeared into the snowy night, Andrei remained at the table, his coffee growing cold as he grappled with the implications of what he'd learned. The pieces were falling into place, but the complete picture still eluded him. And time, he knew, was running out.

Across town, in a spartanly furnished office at KGB headquarters, Viktor Orlov sat hunched over his desk, a half-empty bottle of vodka at his elbow. Spread before him were reports on Andrei Novikov's activities - carefully detailed accounts of his movements, his interactions, his work at the ice rink.

Orlov's eyes, bloodshot from lack of sleep and too much alcohol, scanned the documents for the hundredth time. There was nothing, absolutely nothing, that conclusively pointed to Novikov being anything other than what he claimed to be. His background checked out, his behavior was consistent with his cover story, and even his performance at the ice rink was exemplary.

And yet... Orlov couldn't shake the nagging feeling that something was off. It was there in the way Novikov carried himself, in the sharpness of his gaze that spoke of a man constantly on alert. These were traits Orlov recognized, traits he saw in the mirror every day.

With a growl of frustration, Orlov slammed his fist on the desk, sending papers fluttering to the floor. He was missing something, he was sure of it. And every day that passed without him uncovering the truth felt like another failure, another stain on the Orlov family name.

The portrait of his father, stern and proud in his military uniform, seemed to glare down at him from the wall. Orlov met the painted eyes, his jaw clenching. "I will find the truth, Father," he muttered. "I will restore our honor."

The shrill ring of the telephone cut through Orlov's brooding. He snatched up the receiver, barking a curt greeting. As he listened, his eyes widened, a predatory gleam igniting in their depths. "Are you certain? ... I see. Keep this quiet for now. I'll handle it personally."

Orlov hung up, a grim smile playing at the corners of his mouth. Perhaps the break he needed had finally arrived.

At the Kirov ice rink, chaos reigned. Players huddled in small groups, their voices a mix of shock and speculation. The head coach, a bear of a man named Dmitri Volkov, had just been escorted from the premises, his face a mask of rage and humiliation.

Andrei stood to the side, his face carefully neutral as he observed the unfolding drama. Volkov's firing had come as a shock to everyone - officially due to the team's poor performance and rumors of a drinking problem. But Andrei knew better. He'd seen the way Volkov had been watching him, the growing suspicion in the coach's eyes. Had Volkov stumbled onto something he shouldn't have?

Before Andrei could ponder this further, he felt a hand on his shoulder. He turned to find the rink's owner, a portly man named Yegor Kuznetsov, looking at him with an expression of desperate hope.

"Novikov," Kuznetsov said, his voice low and urgent. "Congratulations, due to unfortunate events, Volkov is terminated. The regional championships are just weeks away, and we're without a coach. You've shown remarkable insight into the game. You are now his replacement as coach."

Andrei's mind raced. This was an unexpected development, one that could either be a golden opportunity or a deadly trap. As coach, he'd have unprecedented access to all areas of the rink, including those mysterious restricted sections. But it would also put him squarely in the spotlight, increasing his risk of exposure.

For a moment, Andrei allowed himself to feel the weight of his alias, of the life he'd constructed here in Kirov. He thought of Taisiya, of the missing agents, of the deadly game of cat and mouse he was playing with Orlov. Then, decision made, he met Kuznetsov's gaze.

"It would be an honor, Mr. Kuznetsov," Andrei said, infusing his voice with just the right mix of surprise and determination. "I'll do my best not to let you down."

As Kuznetsov clapped him on the back and turned to announce the decision to the team, Andrei felt a chill that had nothing to do with the ice beneath his feet. He'd just raised the stakes of his mission exponentially. Now, more than ever, he was walking a tightrope between discovery and success.

The players gathered around, their faces a mix of uncertainty and hope as they looked to their new coach. Andrei straightened his shoulders, already formulating strategies and plays in his mind. But beneath it all, a single thought echoed: the clock was ticking, and the real game was only just beginning.

Chapter 11: Betrayal

The weight of his new responsibilities as interim coach pressed down on Andrei's shoulders as he navigated the bustling streets of Kirov. A convoy of military trucks rumbled past, their presence a constant reminder of the ever-watchful Soviet state. The familiar sign of the café where he and Taisiya often met came into view, its neon glow flickering against the gathering dusk. A knot of dread tightened in Andrei's stomach as he approached.

Andrei paused at the entrance, his hand on the door handle. Through the frosted glass, he could see Taisiya's silhouette at their usual table, her fingers drumming an impatient rhythm. He took a deep breath, steeling himself, and pushed the door open.

The warmth of the café enveloped him, along with the rich aroma of coffee and freshly baked pastries. Taisiya looked up as he approached, her smile faltering as she caught the tension in his posture.

"You're late," she said, her tone light but her eyes searching his face. "And you look like you've seen a ghost."

Andrei slid into the seat across from her, his back to the wall as always, giving him a clear view of the entire café. "Sorry," he murmured, his voice low. "It's been... an interesting day."

Taisiya leaned forward, her brow furrowing. "What's happened? Is it about the Yankees logo?"

Andrei shook his head, his fingers tightening around the coffee cup a waitress had silently placed before him. "No, it's not that. It's... something else. Something I need to tell you."

The tension in the air thickened as Andrei struggled to find the right words. Taisiya's eyes narrowed, her posture stiffening as she sensed the gravity of the moment.

"Taisiya," Andrei began, his voice barely above a whisper, "I've been made interim coach of the hockey team."

For a moment, silence reigned. Taisiya's face cycled through a range of emotions – surprise, confusion, and then, slowly, a dawning realization that morphed into anger.

"Coach?" she hissed, leaning closer to avoid being overheard. "How? When? And why am I only hearing about this now?"

Andrei raised his hands in a placating gesture. "It just happened. Volkov was fired, and they asked me to step in. I saw an opportunity and I took it. This could be huge for our... project."

But Taisiya wasn't mollified. Her eyes flashed dangerously as she processed the information. "Wait a minute," she said, her voice low and tight with suppressed fury. "Coach? Just like that, they made you coach? What aren't you telling me, Andrei?"

The color drained from Andrei's face as he realized his mistake. He'd been so focused on sharing his new position, he'd forgotten that he'd never told Taisiya about his role at the rink.

"I... I can explain," he started, but Taisiya cut him off with a sharp gesture.

"Explain? Explain how you've been lying to me this entire time? How many other secrets are you keeping, Andrei?"

Her words hit Andrei like a physical blow. He could see the hurt and betrayal etched across Taisiya's face, and it tore at him in a way he hadn't expected.

"Taisiya, please," he pleaded, his voice barely above a whisper. "You have to understand. The less you knew, the safer you were. I was trying to protect you."

But Taisiya wasn't having it. She leaned back, crossing her arms over her chest, her eyes cold. "Protect me? By lying to me? By keeping me in the dark about everything?"

Andrei opened his mouth to respond, but Taisiya wasn't finished. Her next words came out in a rush, as if she'd been holding them back for too long.

"And now I find out you're not just working at the rink, but you're the coach? Do you have any idea what that means? You're working for them, Andrei. For the very people I've been trying to escape from my entire life!"

The pain and betrayal in Taisiya's voice cut Andrei to the core. He realized, with a sinking feeling, that he'd underestimated the depth of her feelings, both for him and about her situation.

"Taisiya," he said, reaching across the table to take her hand, but she pulled away. "This isn't what you think. I'm not working for them, I'm... I'm working against them. From the inside."

Taisiya's eyes widened, a mix of disbelief and dawning comprehension crossing her face. "What are you saying?"

Andrei glanced around the café, making sure no one was paying them undue attention. When he spoke again, his voice was so low Taisiya had to lean in to hear him.

"The coaching position, it's perfect. I'll have access to parts of the rink I couldn't get to before. I can find out what they're really up to, maybe even find a way to get you out."

For a moment, hope flickered in Taisiya's eyes. But it was quickly extinguished, replaced by a weariness that made her look years older.

"How can I believe you?" she asked, her voice trembling. "How do I know this isn't just another lie?"

Andrei felt as if the ground was crumbling beneath him. He'd known this conversation would be difficult, but he hadn't anticipated the depth of Taisiya's sense of betrayal. He realized, with a sinking feeling, that he'd jeopardized not just their alliance, but something far more precious – her trust.

As he sat there, grappling for words that could bridge the chasm he'd unwittingly created, Andrei became acutely aware of the precariousness of his position. The café, once a haven, now felt exposed. Every patron was a potential threat, every whispered conversation a possible report to the KGB.

And Taisiya, the one person he'd allowed himself to trust in this frozen wasteland of secrets and lies, was looking at him as if he were a stranger. The weight of his mission, the lives at stake, the global implications of his success or failure – all of it paled in comparison to the hurt in her eyes.

In that moment, Andrei realized that he'd reached a crossroads. The path forward was fraught with danger, not just from external threats, but from the very real possibility of losing the one ally he couldn't bear to be without. As the silence stretched between them, heavy with unspoken accusations and desperate justifications, Andrei knew that his next words could determine not just the fate of his mission, but the course of his life.

Andrei leaned forward, his voice low and urgent. "Taisiya, listen to me. I'm telling you this now because I've finally secured the position. This isn't just about hockey - it's our chance to uncover what's really happening at the rink."

Taisiya's eyes narrowed, skepticism etched in every line of her face. "And how exactly does you being coach help our 'shared goals'?" The last words dripped with sarcasm.

"Think about it," Andrei pressed on, his fingers drumming a nervous rhythm on the tabletop. "As coach, I'll have access to areas of the rink that were off-limits before. The restricted sections, the late-night meetings - I can find out what they're hiding."

A flicker of interest crossed Taisiya's face, but it was quickly replaced by a scowl. "And what about me? Where do I fit into this grand plan of yours?"

The question hung in the air between them, heavy with unspoken implications. Andrei felt the weight of it, the delicate balance he was trying to maintain between his mission and his growing feelings for Taisiya.

"You're essential to this," he said, his voice softening. "Your connections, your knowledge of the town - we're in this together, Taisiya. I couldn't do this without you."

Taisiya's laugh was bitter, cutting through the tense atmosphere. "Together? You've been lying to me from the start, Andrei. How can we be in this together when I don't even know who you really are?"

The words stung, but Andrei recognized the truth in them. He'd kept so much from her, always justifying it as necessary for the mission. But now, faced with the hurt in her eyes, he realized the cost of his secrecy.

"You're right," he admitted, the words feeling foreign on his tongue. "I've kept things from you. But it was always to protect you, to keep you safe."

Taisiya's eyes flashed. "I don't need your protection, Andrei. I need the truth."

The conversation spiraled, emotions long suppressed bubbling to the surface. Taisiya's fears of betrayal clashed with Andrei's ingrained habit of secrecy. Their voices, though kept low, trembled with the intensity of their feelings.

"Do you have any idea what it's like?" Taisiya hissed, her knuckles white around her coffee cup. "To live every day wondering if this is it, if today's the day they come for me? And now I find out you're one of them-"

"I'm not one of them," Andrei cut in, his own anger flaring. "Everything I've done, everything I'm doing, is to bring them down. To give people like you a chance at freedom."

The word 'freedom' hung between them, a tangible thing. Taisiya's expression softened slightly, a glimmer of understanding in her eyes.

"And what about us?" she asked, her voice barely above a whisper. "Is that part of your mission too?"

Andrei felt as if the ground had dropped out from under him. He'd been so focused on the mission, on maintaining his cover, that he'd never allowed himself to fully confront his feelings for Taisiya.

"No," he said finally, his voice rough. "That's... that's real. Whatever else I've hidden, whatever lies I've told - how I feel about you isn't one of them."

A long moment of silence stretched between them. The bustle of the café faded into the background as they stared at each other, moments of tension and unspoken feelings hanging in the balance.

Finally, Taisiya sighed, her shoulders slumping slightly. "I want to believe you, Andrei. But I don't know if I can trust you."

Andrei nodded, understanding the fragility of the moment. "I know. But I'm asking you to try. Let me prove to you that we're on the same side."

Taisiya studied him for a long moment before giving a curt nod. "Alright. But no more secrets. If we're really in this together, I need to know everything."

As they left the café, their alliance restored but fundamentally changed, Andrei felt the weight of his promises pressing down on him. He'd opened a door he wasn't sure he could close, and the consequences could be deadly for both of them.

Over the next weeks, Andrei threw himself into his role as coach with a fervor that surprised even him. He ran drills, developed strategies, and pushed the team harder than they'd ever been pushed before. But beneath the surface of every interaction, every decision, lay his true purpose.

He used his new position to explore previously restricted areas of the rink, his eyes and ears constantly alert for any sign of the missing agents or the secret project. Late at night, long after the team had gone home, Andrei would prowl the darkened corridors, picking locks and searching for clues.

Each discovery, each scrap of information, he carefully cataloged and shared with Taisiya during clandestine meetings. Their relationship, though strained, had taken on a new intensity. The shared danger, the thrill of uncovering the truth, bound them together in ways neither had anticipated.

As Andrei stood at the rink's edge one evening, watching his team practice, he felt a chill that had nothing to do with the ice. He was close to something big; he could feel it. But with each step closer to the truth, the noose around his neck tightened. The game was reaching its climax, and Andrei knew that soon, very soon, he would have to make a move that would either save them all or doom them to failure.

Chapter 12:
The Long Game

The sharp crack of hockey sticks against pucks echoed through the ice rink as Andrei barked out orders to his team. His voice reverberated across the empty stands, but his mind was far from the practice drills. Over the past week, he'd noticed a subtle shift in the atmosphere around the rink. More unfamiliar faces lingered in the lobby, security checks at the entrance had intensified, and there was an unmistakable feeling of eyes constantly watching his every move.

As the team filed off the ice, Andrei's gaze swept the perimeter of the rink. There, in the shadows of the upper tier, he caught a glimpse of a figure quickly ducking out of sight. His jaw clenched. The KGB was closing in, and his window of opportunity was shrinking fast.

Back in his small office, Andrei sat at his desk, fingers steepled under his chin as he contemplated his next move. The stakes were too high for simple evasion now. It was time to go on the offensive.

With deliberate care, Andrei pulled out a sheaf of papers from his briefcase. To the untrained eye, they looked like ordinary hockey strategies and player statistics. But hidden within were carefully crafted falsehoods – hints of non-existent operatives, suggestions of clandestine meetings that never occurred. He shuffled through them, a ghost of a smile playing on his lips.

The next morning, Andrei arrived at the rink earlier than usual. He made a show of working at his desk, the falsified documents spread out before him. Then, with an exaggerated gesture of frustration, he swept the papers into his briefcase and hurried out, "accidentally" dropping a few sheets on the floor in his haste.

As he rounded the corner, Andrei paused, his back pressed against the cold concrete wall. He heard the soft creak of his office door opening, followed by the rustle of papers being hastily collected. A triumphant murmur reached his ears, and he allowed himself a moment of satisfaction. The bait had been taken.

Later that week, Andrei found himself at a state dinner, rubbing shoulders with local party officials and military brass. The air was thick with cigarette smoke and thinly veiled political maneuvering. As he navigated the crowd, a conversation caught his ear – two high-ranking officials discussing recent security concerns.

Andrei smoothly inserted himself into their circle, a glass of vodka in hand and a carefully constructed expression of concern on his face. "Forgive my intrusion, comrades," he said, his voice low and conspiratorial, "but I couldn't help overhearing. These security issues – they wouldn't happen to be related to the recent... disturbances in Leningrad, would they?"

The officials exchanged wary glances. "What disturbances?" one asked, his bushy eyebrows furrowing.

Andrei affected a look of surprise. "You haven't heard? There are whispers of unrest, echoes of the old Kronstadt rebellion. Some say there are still those who cling to Trotsky's ideals, working to undermine us from within."

He watched as the seeds of doubt took root in their minds. The conversation quickly turned to discussions of internal threats and the need for increased vigilance against ideological corruption. Andrei sipped his vodka, inwardly pleased. The spotlight of suspicion had been neatly shifted away from him and onto a non-existent internal threat.

As the weeks wore on, Andrei knew he needed to take more drastic action to secure his position. The constant pressure of surveillance was taking its toll, and he needed to provide the KGB with something that would throw them off his scent for good.

The plan he concocted was risky, but necessary. He arranged to meet Taisiya at a busy café in the heart of Kirov, knowing full well that KGB agents would be watching. As they sat down, Andrei leaned in close, his voice barely above a whisper.

"Taisiya, I need you to trust me. What happens next is not real, but it needs to look convincing. Can you do that?"

Confusion flashed across Taisiya's face, but she gave an almost imperceptible nod. Andrei took a deep breath, then launched into a tirade, his voice rising with each word.

"How could you be so careless?" he hissed, loud enough for nearby patrons to hear. "Do you have any idea what you've done?"

Taisiya, catching on quickly, matched his intensity. "Me? You're the one who's been acting suspiciously! Maybe if you'd trust me enough to tell me what's really going on-"

Their argument escalated, drawing the attention of everyone in the café. Accusations flew back and forth, each more outlandish than the last. Finally, Andrei stood abruptly, his chair scraping loudly against the floor.

"I can't do this anymore," he declared, his voice thick with feigned emotion. "It's over, Taisiya. All of it."

As he stormed out of the café, Andrei caught sight of a familiar face in the crowd – one of Orlov's men, hastily scribbling notes. A grim satisfaction settled in his chest. The performance had had its intended audience.

That night, long after the rink had emptied of players and staff, Andrei prowled the darkened corridors. His investigation had led him to believe that there was more to this facility than met the eye, and he was determined to uncover its secrets.

As he ran his hands along the walls of a back storage room, Andrei's fingers caught on a barely perceptible seam. His heart rate quickened as he applied pressure, feeling the wall give way slightly. With a soft click, a hidden compartment sprung open.

Inside, illuminated by the beam of Andrei's flashlight, was a stack of blueprints. He pulled them out with trembling hands, his eyes widening as he unrolled the first sheet. The designs were like nothing he'd ever seen before – complex schematics for what looked like advanced weapons systems, far beyond anything the Soviets were supposed to possess.

As Andrei pored over the blueprints, a chill ran down his spine. This was it – the missing piece of the puzzle. Whatever was happening here at the rink, whatever the missing agents had been forced to work on, it was bigger and more dangerous than he'd ever imagined.

The sound of a door slamming somewhere in the distance jolted Andrei back to reality. He quickly replaced the blueprints, his mind racing. He'd found what he'd been looking for, but the discovery only raised more questions. As he slipped out of the storage room and melted into the shadows of the corridor, Andrei knew that the true game was only just beginning.

The blueprints he'd found had confirmed his suspicions about the ice rink's secret purpose, but they'd also raised the stakes exponentially. He knew he was playing a dangerous game, and the margin for error was shrinking by the day.

Little did Andrei know, across town, his nemesis was closing in. In his dimly lit office, Viktor Orlov slammed his fist on the desk, sending papers flying. The dim light cast long shadows across his haggard face. Weeks of surveillance, interrogations, and sleepless nights had yielded nothing concrete on Andrei Novikov. Yet the gnawing suspicion in Orlov's gut refused to subside.

"He's too perfect," Orlov muttered, eyes scanning the scattered reports. "No one's background checks out this cleanly."

A knock at the door interrupted his brooding. A junior officer entered, face pale. "Sir, we've intercepted a message. It's... it's about Novikov."

Orlov snatched the paper, eyes devouring its contents. His breath caught. The message, though coded, hinted at Novikov's involvement in something far beyond coaching hockey.

"Get me everything on Novikov's movements for the past month," Orlov barked. "Every person he's talked to, every place he's been. I want it all!" He further added, "Also get me the newspapers, we need to see if the Americans are talking about their missing agents"

As Orlov's net tightened, Andrei felt the pressure mounting. He needed a distraction, something big enough to divert the KGB's attention. The answer came in the form of a seemingly innocuous newspaper article about tensions with a neighboring satellite state.

At the next party gathering, Andrei carefully maneuvered conversations towards the topic. He dropped subtle hints about potential unrest, playing on the officials' fears of losing control.

"I've heard whispers," he murmured to a high-ranking party member, voice low and concerned. "Dissent spreading from the factories to the universities. If it's not contained..."

The official's eyes widened. "You're certain?"

Andrei nodded gravely. "I fear it may already be too late."

The rumors spread like wildfire. Within days, the KGB was scrambling to investigate the non-existent threat, resources diverted from other operations – including the surveillance on Andrei.

He allowed himself a moment of relief, but knew it was temporary. The game was far from over.

In his office, Orlov pored over the latest reports, frustration etched in every line of his face. The wild goose chase about civil unrest had set his investigation back weeks. He was about to call it a night when a small detail caught his eye.

Buried in a report about Novikov's background was a discrepancy – a date that didn't match previous records. Heart pounding, Orlov dug deeper, cross-referencing files and interrogation transcripts.

As the pieces fell into place, a chill ran down Orlov's spine. The inconsistencies, the too-perfect cover story, the convenient distractions – it all pointed to one inescapable conclusion.

Andrei Novikov was not who he claimed to be.

Orlov's hand shook as he reached for the phone. "Get me a direct line to Moscow," he ordered. "And put out an alert. Novikov is not to leave Kirov under any circumstances."

As he waited for the connection, Orlov's gaze fell on the photo of his father. "I've got him, Father," he whispered. "I've finally got him."

The phone crackled to life. "Moscow here. Report, Comrade Orlov."

Orlov took a deep breath, savoring the moment he'd fought so hard for. “Sir, I have evidence that Andrei Novikov is an American spy."

The words hung in the air, heavy with implication. In that moment, Viktor Orlov knew that everything was about to change. The hunt was on, and this time, he would not let his prey escape.

Chapter 13:
Love in a Cold Climate

The static-filled voice of Radio Moscow crackled through Andrei's small apartment as he methodically cleaned his hockey equipment. His hands moved automatically over the gear, but his attention was fixed on the news broadcast.

"...successful test of the American Titan missile has escalated tensions between the United States and the Soviet Union. The Supreme Soviet has issued a statement condemning this provocative action..."

Andrei's jaw tightened. The timing couldn't be worse. Through his apartment window, he observed six KGB vehicles patrolling the street below - twice the usual number. The streets of Kirov had transformed overnight, crawling with agents attempting to look inconspicuous in their dark coats and stern expressions.

The radio crackled again. "In related news, the Ministry of Defense announces increased security measures across all major industrial centers..."

Andrei switched off the radio, his mind racing. The KGB's heightened presence meant his window of opportunity was shrinking rapidly. He needed to act soon, but one wrong move now could prove fatal.

The next morning found Andrei in the market square, a shopping list in his hand and keen awareness in his eyes. He moved from stall to stall, appearing to examine produce while actually documenting the KGB's patrol patterns. Two agents at the north entrance, rotating every thirty minutes. Three more circulating through the crowd, their telltale stiff postures giving them away.

From her position at the bakery window, Taisiya wiped the same spot on the counter repeatedly, her eyes tracking the movements of unfamiliar faces through the square. A new team had arrived yesterday - four men with the unmistakable bearing of KGB operatives, their presence adding another layer of complexity to an already precarious situation.

Andrei approached the bakery, timing his entrance to coincide with a gap in the patrols. The bell above the door chimed as he entered.

"The usual, please," he said, his voice carrying just the right amount of casual friendliness. "And perhaps one of those new loaves I saw in the window?"

Taisiya nodded, understanding the coded request. She reached for a specific loaf, one marked with three small cuts on top - their signal for a meeting at the third location, midnight. "Fresh this morning," she replied, wrapping the bread carefully. "Though I'm afraid we're running low on flour. The delivery schedule has been... irregular lately."

Andrei caught her meaning - their usual communication routes were compromised. "Perhaps you should place an advertisement in the paper," he suggested, maintaining his pleasant customer facade. "I'm sure there are other suppliers."

That evening, Andrei spotted Taisiya's carefully worded advertisement in the local newspaper: "Quality flour needed for local bakery. Delivery after dark preferred. Inquire within." To anyone else, it appeared to be a simple business notice. To Andrei, it confirmed their midnight meeting and warned of heavy surveillance along their primary route.

They had developed dozens of such signals over the weeks - a certain way of arranging pastries in the window, specific phrases dropped into casual conversation, even the position of Taisiya's flower box could convey vital information. It was a delicate dance of deception, every move calculated and precise.

The breakthrough came three days later. Andrei was working late at the rink, supposedly reviewing game strategies, when voices drifted from the restricted area. He pressed himself against the wall, straining to hear.

"The guidance system must be ready by the fifteenth," a gruff voice insisted. "Moscow won't tolerate any more delays."

"It's not that simple," another voice responded, American-accented and strained. "The calibrations for the new coordinates are extremely delicate. One mistake could send the missile hundreds of miles off course."

Andrei's breath caught. The missing agents, the mysterious blueprints, the increased security - it all clicked into place. The Soviets weren't just developing a new weapons system; they were forcing the captured American agents to help perfect it.

The coordinates mentioned matched the location he'd discovered in the blueprints. They were planning a test launch, and soon. The implications were staggering. If the Soviets successfully tested an advanced guidance system, it would shift the balance of power significantly.

As Andrei slipped away from the conversation, his mind was already formulating a plan. The fifteenth - that gave him less than a week to act. He needed to get word to Arthur, organize an extraction for the captured agents, and somehow prevent the test launch.

The stakes had never been higher. One misstep now wouldn't just mean his own capture and execution - it could spark an international crisis. As he left the ice rink, Andrei's steps were measured and calm, betraying none of the urgency churning inside him. The game had entered its final, most dangerous phase, and the clock was ticking.

The evening bells of St. Nicholas Church tolled across Kirov as Andrei knelt in the shadows of the confessional. His fingers traced the underside of the wooden bench until he found the small crevice. There, he deposited a tightly folded piece of paper containing the critical intelligence about the weapons test. This was the first step in a complex chain that would eventually reach Arthur back in Buffalo.

The system was elaborate but necessary. From Kirov to Buffalo, the message would pass through multiple hands. First, the elderly flower seller who swept the church steps each morning would collect it. Then to the deaf warehouse worker who delivered paper to the local printer. The message would then move to Moscow with a traveling salesman, where it would be transmitted to Arthur through diplomatic channels. Each person knew only their immediate contact, none aware of the full communication chain or its ultimate destination.

Two days later, Andrei found Arthur's response tucked inside his morning newspaper, having traveled the same careful route in reverse. The message was brief but clear: "Proceed with extraction. Priority: agents and blueprints. Prevent test if possible. Assets enroute."

That evening, Andrei met Taisiya in the back room of the bakery, the hum of the evening rush masking their conversation. Her face paled as he laid out the full scope of the mission.

"The men they're holding," Andrei explained, his voice barely above a whisper, "they're American spies with a history in Weapons Research Division. The Soviets are forcing them to develop an advanced missile guidance system. If they succeed..."

"It would change everything," Taisiya finished, understanding dawning in her eyes. "But why tell me this now?"

"Because what we're about to attempt is incredibly dangerous. You need to know exactly what you're risking." Andrei's eyes met hers, holding nothing back. "If we're caught, it won't just be prison. They'll execute us as spies."

Taisiya's hands trembled slightly, but her voice remained steady. "I've lived under their shadow my entire life, Andrei. If there's a chance to strike back, to help those men and maybe find my own freedom..." She straightened her shoulders. "I'm in. Whatever it takes."

Over the next two days, they worked feverishly to plan their escape routes. Andrei spread a detailed map of Kirov across his kitchen table, marking primary and secondary evacuation paths. "The main route takes us north through the industrial district," he explained, tracing the path with his finger. "But we'll need alternatives."

Taisiya nodded, pointing to several locations. "I know people here, here, and here - families who've lost loved ones to the regime. They'll help us without asking questions." She hesitated, then added, "And there's an old hunting cabin in the woods, about fifty kilometers east. It's been abandoned since the war."

They established emergency protocols for every scenario they could imagine. If separated, they would meet at one of three predetermined locations. If communication was compromised, they had a series of visual signals. If one was captured, the other would proceed alone.

The timeline was brutally tight. With the weapons test scheduled for the fifteenth, they had just three days left to finalize and execute their plan. Andrei spread his notebook across the table, detailing each phase of the operation.

"The test happens at dawn on the fifteenth," he said, his voice low and urgent. "We need to move the night before. That gives us exactly three days to get everything in place."

Taisiya nodded, understanding the pressure of the countdown. "The uniforms and passes will be ready tomorrow.

My contact at the laundry service has already started working on them."

"Good. We'll need the medical supplies by the fourteenth. If your cousin at the hospital can't get them all, we have to know now."

They methodically worked through each element of the plan. The route to the restricted area, the timing of the guard rotations, the exact location of the scientists based on their intelligence - everything had to be perfect. There would be no second chances.

"Once we move," Andrei explained, "the entire KGB apparatus will descend on us. We'll have minutes, maybe seconds, to get clear before they realize what's happening."

As the evening wore on, the reality of their situation settled over them. In just three days, they would attempt something that could either change the course of the Cold War or end their lives. The countdown had begun, and every passing hour brought them closer to the point of no return.

The next morning, Andrei noticed the shift immediately. The usual KGB patrols had altered their routes, clustering more heavily around the ice rink and its surrounding areas. At the corner of Marx Street, a new figure caught his attention - a tall officer whose military bearing set him apart from the typical agents. Unlike the others who attempted to blend in, this one carried his authority openly. The other agents deferred to him with a mix of respect and fear. *Novak*, Andrei heard one of them murmur.

Through their carefully established channels, Taisiya's report confirmed his observations. The bakery had acquired a new regular - a KGB agent who lingered for hours over a single coffee, his eyes never leaving the street. More concerning were Novak's occasional visits, his questions about regular customers carrying an edge of calculated purpose.

The final confirmation from Arthur arrived hidden within the morning newspaper's classifieds: "Winter wheat prices stable through season's end." The seemingly innocent agricultural report carried their go-ahead signal. There would be no further communication until after the operation.

Taisiya had done her part, securing the necessary documents through her network of trusted contacts. Travel papers, work permits, identification cards - each forgery crafted to withstand the most rigorous inspection. Medical supplies lay hidden within innocent bread deliveries, ready for the next day's execution of their plan.

The bell above the bakery door chimed as Andrei entered for their final coordination meeting. Everything appeared normal - customers chatting over coffee, Taisiya behind the counter, the daily rhythm of commerce unchanged. But beneath the surface, tension crackled like static electricity.

"The usual, please," Andrei said, his voice steady despite the hammering of his heart. Taisiya nodded; her movements deliberate as she wrapped a loaf of bread. Her hands trembled slightly - the only visible sign of her nerves.

"Beautiful weather for this time of year," she commented, their predetermined signal that everything was in place.

"Yes, perfect for a walk in the park," Andrei replied, completing the code.

The next few seconds unfolded with brutal efficiency. The bell above the door chimed again, but this time it wasn't a customer. Heavy boots thudded against the wooden floor. Novak's voice cut through the quiet murmur of the bakery.

"Nobody moves!"

KGB agents poured through both entrances, their movements precise and coordinated. Customers screamed and scattered, but Andrei remained still, his mind racing. This was no random raid - they knew exactly who they were looking for.

Novak approached; his face impassive. "Andrei Novikov," he said, the name sounding like an accusation.

Strong hands grabbed Andrei's arms, pinning them behind his back. As they led him toward the door, Andrei caught one last glimpse of Taisiya through the bakery window. She stood frozen behind the counter, her face a mask of horror and despair. Their eyes met for a brief moment - a moment that contained all their unspoken words, their shared dreams of freedom, their doomed plans.

Then rough hands shoved him into a waiting car, and Taisiya disappeared from view. As the car pulled away, Andrei's mind whirled with questions. How had they known? Who had betrayed them? And what would happen to Taisiya?

The last thing he saw before they blindfolded him was Novak's satisfied smile in the rearview mirror. The game was over, but Andrei couldn't shake the feeling that he still didn't know all the players or their true roles in this deadly match of cat and mouse.

Chapter 14: The Interrogator

The hood was ripped from Andrei's head, leaving him blinking against the harsh fluorescent lights of the KGB detention facility. An iron grip shoved him forward, his shoulders aching from being bound behind his back during the drive. The processing room reeked of disinfectant and fear.

"Strip," a guard barked in Russian, punctuating the command with a sharp jab to Andrei's ribs.

As Andrei complied, two guards searched his clothes with methodical brutality, ripping seams and tearing linings. A third guard raised his baton when Andrei didn't move fast enough, but a sharp voice cut through the room.

"That's enough, Comrade."

Novak stood in the doorway, his presence immediately altering the atmosphere. The guard's baton froze mid-swing, then lowered slowly. Novak's eyes swept over the scene, his expression unreadable.

"We're not barbarians," Novak continued, his tone almost casual. "Process him properly. No unnecessary force."

The guards exchanged confused glances but complied. Their handling remained rough but stopped short of outright brutality. Andrei noted this departure from standard KGB protocol, filing it away as an anomaly to be analyzed later.

The cell they threw him into was a concrete box, six feet by eight, with a metal cot bolted to the wall and a toilet in the corner. No window, just a single bulb burning overhead. The door, solid steel with a small observation slot, clanged shut with crushing finality.

Andrei sat on the cot, his training kicking in as he assessed his situation. The guards' shifts changed every four hours - he could tell by the different footsteps in the corridor. Each brought their own style of intimidation. One preferred to slam his baton against the door at random intervals. Another would slide the observation slot open and stare silently for long minutes.

Then Novak would appear, his measured footsteps distinctive in the corridor. The abuse would cease, the psychological tactics would pause. It was as if the entire facility held its breath when Novak was present.

The first interrogation came after what Andrei estimated to be twelve hours of detention. Two guards escorted him to a room dominated by a metal table, recording equipment prominently displayed in one corner. Three KGB officers sat along one wall; their faces set in identical masks of stern disapproval.

The door opened again, and Novak entered with an almost theatrical flourish. His presence commanded immediate attention, the other officers straightening unconsciously in their chairs.

"Comrade Novikov," Novak said, settling into the chair across from Andrei. "Or should I say, Coach Novikov? Interesting strategy you developed for improving the team's defensive play. That neutral zone trap - quite innovative."

Andrei's blood ran cold. That particular strategy had been part of his coded message to his handler, discussed only in the most private of circumstances. How could Novak know those specific details?

"Tell me," Novak continued, fiddling with the recording equipment, "was it before or after developing these strategies that you planned the weapons facility break-in?"

A red light on the recorder flickered and died. Novak frowned, tapping the machine. "Technical difficulties," he muttered. Then, almost casually, he added, "Your mission briefing was quite thorough. Especially the part about using the maintenance schedule as cover. Very clever."

Andrei fought to keep his face neutral, but his mind raced. That detail had been part of his secure communication with his handler, shared through their most protected channels. Only two people knew those specifics - Andrei himself, and the person he reported to.

The recorder's light blinked back to life. Novak's questioning suddenly shifted, becoming almost helpful. "You maintained your cover well at the ice rink. Multiple witnesses can attest to your dedication to coaching. Why, just last week, you spent six hours running drills with the team. Isn't that correct?"

Andrei recognized the lifeline being thrown. "Yes," he replied carefully. "We were preparing for the regional championships."

"And your presence at the bakery? Merely a customer, I assume?"

"I enjoy fresh bread," Andrei said, catching on to the pattern. "The bakery was convenient to my apartment."

The other KGB officers shifted uncomfortably, clearly confused by Novak's approach. One started to speak, but Novak silenced him with a sharp glance.

"Of course," Novak continued smoothly. "And the multiple witnesses who can confirm your regular purchases and normal customer behavior would support that statement, wouldn't they?"

The recorder sputtered again, its light dying. Novak sighed theatrically. "These machines. So unreliable. Perhaps we should take a brief recess while it's repaired."

As the other officers filed out, Novak remained seated, his eyes locked on Andrei. The moment stretched, heavy with unspoken understanding. Something was happening here, something beyond a standard KGB interrogation. But what game was Novak playing, and why?

The questioning resumed once the other officers returned, but now Andrei watched it with new eyes. Every technical malfunction seemed precisely timed. Every question contained a built-in escape route. Every piece of damaging information was revealed when the recorder conveniently failed.

Novak was orchestrating something elaborate, but to what end? And how did he know so much about Andrei's private conversations with Arthur? As the interrogation continued, one thing became clear - nothing about this situation was what it seemed.

The interrogation dragged on, each hour bringing new layers of confusion for Andrei. Novak leaned back in his chair; his posture deceptively relaxed.

"Your mission planning was quite thorough," Novak remarked, just as the recorder's red light flickered out again. "Almost as if you had inside knowledge of our security protocols. The kind of information that only someone in a very... particular position would know."

The implication hung in the air, heavy and unsettling. Andrei kept his face neutral, but his mind raced. Those security details had been part of his briefing, information provided through channels he'd trusted implicitly.

"Strange," Novak continued, making no move to fix the recorder, "how certain people always seem to know exactly when to make their moves. When to push forward, when to pull back." He paused, a slight smile playing at his lips. "When to sacrifice their pieces."

Each word felt calculated, designed to plant seeds of doubt. The recorder hummed back to life, and Novak smoothly shifted topics, but the damage was done. Questions began to form in Andrei's mind, unwanted but impossible to ignore.

As the hours stretched on, Andrei noticed a pattern emerging. Every time the recording equipment "malfunctioned," Novak's questions took on a different tone. More pointed, yet somehow less threatening. During one such "technical difficulty," Novak leaned forward, his voice dropping to barely above a whisper.

"Those who trust blindly often find themselves standing alone when the curtain falls," he said, the words carrying the weight of both warning and revelation.

Andrei began adapting his responses to this strange rhythm of interrogation. When the recorder worked, he stuck to his cover story, playing the role of the confused coach. During the convenient malfunctions, he listened carefully to Novak's cryptic statements, searching for hidden meanings.

"Some loyalties," Novak remarked during one such unrecorded moment, "run deeper than national borders. Others..." he paused significantly, "only run as deep as necessity demands."

The pattern continued until late in the evening, when Novak suddenly straightened in his chair. "Leave us," he commanded the other officers. "I'll handle this phase personally."

Once alone, the atmosphere in the room shifted. Novak's theatrical demeanor dropped slightly, revealing something harder, more focused beneath.

"The next forty-eight hours will be critical," he said, his voice low and urgent. "Events have been set in motion that cannot be stopped. When the time comes, remember - sometimes the most obvious path is the most dangerous."

Andrei studied Novak's face, searching for any clue to his true motives. The man was clearly playing a deeper game, but to what end? And whose side was he really on?

"The ice rink," Novak continued, "will be heavily guarded tomorrow night. Every entrance, every exit - except one. The kind of oversight that only someone with intimate knowledge of our operations could arrange."

The implications of Novak's words crashed over Andrei like a wave of ice water. Could his handler have actually engineered his capture? Was this all part of some larger plan he wasn't privy to?

As guards led him back to his cell, Andrei's mind churned with possibilities. Every piece of information he'd received, every step of his mission - how much had been compromised? The familiar foundations of his world were cracking, revealing shadows and uncertainties beneath.

In the solitude of his cell, Andrei paced, five steps each way. Novak's words echoed in his head, along with all the subtle hints and implications of the interrogation. The man clearly knew things he shouldn't know, things that only someone with access to the highest levels of mission planning would know.

But more disturbing than what Novak knew was how he chose to use that knowledge. Every revelation seemed carefully crafted; each piece of information delivered with surgical precision. Was he trying to help Andrei, or was this all an elaborate trap?

As night settled over the detention facility, Andrei lay on his cot, staring at the ceiling. The truth felt just out of reach, like a word on the tip of his tongue. Someone had betrayed him - that much was clear. But was it the person he'd trusted most, the one who'd sent him on this mission? And if so, what was Novak's role in this deadly game of chess?

Sleep eluded him as the questions multiplied. Tomorrow would bring new interrogations, new revelations, new doubts. But one thing was certain - nothing about this situation was what it appeared to be, and no one could be trusted completely.

The sound of boots in the corridor signaled the changing of the guard. Andrei closed his eyes, his mind still racing. In the game of espionage, truth was as dangerous as any weapon, and loyalty was a double-edged sword that could cut in any direction. As he finally drifted into an uneasy sleep, one question burned brighter than all the others: In a world of shadows and lies, who was really pulling the strings?

Chapter 15:
The Breaking Point

The fluorescent lights buzzed overhead as two guards marched Andrei down the stark corridor. Two days of interrogation had left him exhausted, but his mind remained sharp, constantly analyzing his situation. The guards stopped abruptly at an intersection, apparently confused about their destination.

Through the momentary pause, voices drifted from a partially open office door. Andrei's heart nearly stopped. He knew that voice - had known it for years.

"His cover was perfect," Novak's voice carried clearly, tinged with amusement. "Almost too perfect, we didn’t do anything wrong with him, right?

"We did what was necessary." Arthur's voice, but different somehow. Subdued. Wrong.

Andrei's blood ran cold. The guards pulled him forward, but those few seconds had changed everything. The familiar voice of his handler, discussing mission details with the KGB officer who'd arrested him - it shattered the foundations of everything Andrei thought he knew.

Later that day, Andrei sat before a panel of KGB officers, his wrists cuffed to a heavy wooden chair. Folders of evidence lay spread across the table - photographs, transcripts, surveillance reports. Novak stood to the side, his presence commanding the room.

"Let us review the facts," the senior officer began. "You arrived in Kirov as an equipment manager, then rapidly advanced to coach position. Quite a remarkable rise."

"Talent finds its level," Andrei replied carefully. "My record speaks for itself."

Novak stepped forward, opening a folder. "Indeed it does. Practice schedules, team rosters, detailed training plans dating back months. Very thorough documentation."

The senior officer frowned. "But your frequent visits to the bakery…"

"Were exactly what they appeared to be," Novak interrupted smoothly. "We have statements from multiple customers confirming Comrade Novikov's regular purchases. Nothing unusual about a man enjoying fresh bread, is there?"

Andrei watched the exchange with growing fascination. Novak was actually helping build his defense, but why?

The evidence mounted in Andrei's favor. Players from the hockey team testified to his dedication as a coach. Local shopkeepers confirmed his regular routines. Even his suspicious movements around the ice rink were explained away by maintenance schedules and coaching duties.

"And what of his meetings with the baker woman?" another officer demanded.

"Ah yes," Novak smiled, producing more documents. "A perfectly natural attraction between two young people. Unless love is now considered suspicious activity?"

The panel shifted uncomfortably. Every potential hole in Andrei's cover had been meticulously plugged, every suspicious action explained away. It was too perfect, too clean - yet none of the other officers seemed to notice or care.

As the hearing concluded, a clerk appeared with release papers, processing them with surprising speed. The senior officer delivered the standard warnings with practiced boredom.

"You will remain under surveillance. Any suspicious activity will result in immediate arrest. Your movements will be restricted to approved areas only."

Andrei nodded, maintaining his relieved but slightly intimidated expression. Inside, his mind raced. This wasn't how KGB investigations typically ended. Something else was at play here.

As the guards prepared to escort him out, Novak stepped forward for a final word.

"Remember, Comrade Novikov," he said, his voice carrying that same strange undertone Andrei had noticed during interrogations, "sometimes the best move in chess isn't the most obvious one. The piece you think is threatening you might actually be protecting you."

Andrei met Novak's gaze, searching for some clue to the man's true motives. But Novak's face remained unreadable, his slight smile revealing nothing.

Minutes later, Andrei stood on the street outside the KGB facility, officially a free man. The weight of what he'd overheard pressed down on him like a physical force. Arthur's voice, discussing mission details with Novak. The too-perfect release. Novak's cryptic warnings.

Nothing made sense, yet everything was falling into place. But into what pattern? And more importantly, with less than twenty-four hours until the weapons test, what was he supposed to do now?

The late afternoon sun cast long shadows across the street as Andrei began walking, his steps measured and calm despite the turmoil in his mind. He was being watched; he knew that with certainty. The game wasn't over - it was merely entering a new, more dangerous phase.

Behind him, in the growing darkness, Novak watched from his office window, that same enigmatic smile playing across his face. The pieces were in motion, the board set for the final game. But who was really playing whom?

The safe house felt smaller than Andrei remembered as he paced its confines, his mind churning with the implications of what he'd overheard. Arthur's voice, discussing mission details with Novak, played on an endless loop in his head. Every shared secret, every confidential plan - how much had been compromised?

Yet Novak's behavior didn't fit the pattern of a simple betrayal. The orchestrated release, the cryptic warnings, the carefully guided questioning - it all pointed to something more complex. But with the weapons test scheduled for tomorrow at dawn, Andrei had no time to unravel the mystery.

He spread the original mission plans across a rickety table, analyzing each element with fresh eyes. The entrance routes, the timing, the backup plans - all potentially compromised. Even the extraction points couldn't be trusted. He'd have to rebuild the entire operation from scratch, with less than twelve hours remaining.

Andrei pulled out a fresh sheet of paper, his pencil moving swiftly as he sketched new approach vectors. The ice rink's security would be heightened after his arrest, but that might work to his advantage. They'd be watching the obvious entry points, expecting a frontal assault.

A soft knock at the door interrupted his planning. Three sharp taps, followed by two slow ones - Taisiya's signal. Andrei opened the door carefully, gun ready behind his back, but it was indeed her. Her eyes met his, relief flickering across her face before she quickly masked it. They allowed themselves one brief embrace - the first since his detention - then stepped apart, reverting to the practiced efficiency their mission demanded. She slipped inside, her face pale but determined.

"The bakery's being watched," she reported without preamble. "But I can still move around. They don't suspect me."

Andrei nodded. "You're our biggest advantage now. They'll be focused on me, expecting me to lead the operation."

"What about the others? The backup team?"

"Can't risk it. Anyone Arthur knew about is potentially compromised." Andrei's jaw tightened. "We do this with the people we know we can trust. Just us and the two others who weren't part of the original briefing."

As if on cue, another knock came - the warehouse worker and the night watchman, their newest recruits. Andrei had specifically kept them off the official mission roster, a precaution that now seemed prescient.

The next hour was spent outlining the new plan. No elaborate schemes, no complex diversions. Simple, direct, with each person having only the information they absolutely needed.

"The weapons test is scheduled for dawn," Andrei explained, pointing to the crude map he'd drawn. "That gives us one shot. The scientists will be brought to the facility tonight for final preparations. That's our window."

Taisiya studied the map. "The delivery entrance?"

"Too obvious. They'll expect that." Andrei traced a different route. "There's a maintenance tunnel, used for accessing the cooling systems. It's tight, barely wide enough for one person, but it connects to the sublevels."

The warehouse worker frowned. "What about the guards?"

"They'll be concentrated around the known entrances. And they'll be watching me." Andrei's lips curved in a grim smile. "Which is exactly what we need."

The plan took shape quickly. Andrei would make himself visible, drawing attention while the others moved into position. Taisiya's role was crucial - she'd use her bakery deliveries as cover to smuggle in essential equipment. The warehouse worker and night watchman would handle the actual extraction, their familiarity with the facility's layout proving invaluable.

"Timing is everything," Andrei stressed. "Once we move, we'll have minutes at most. If anyone gets captured..." He left the sentence unfinished. They all knew the stakes.

As the others left, each taking different routes to avoid surveillance, Andrei returned to fine-tuning the details. Every contingency had to be covered; every possible complication anticipated. Yet questions about Arthur's role continued to nag at him.

Had his handler really betrayed him? Or was this part of some larger plan Andrei couldn't see? And what of Novak's strange behavior? The KGB officer seemed to be playing his own game, but to what end?

Andrei shook his head, forcing the questions aside. Dawn was approaching, and with it, their last chance to stop the weapons test and rescue the captured scientists. The mystery of Arthur's loyalty would have to wait.

He checked his watch - six hours until the mission. Six hours to either succeed or die trying. Outside, the Kirov night pressed against the windows, full of shadows and secrets.

Somewhere in the darkness, Novak was surely watching, waiting to see what move Andrei would make next.

The game was reaching its climax, and the stakes had never been higher. As Andrei made his final preparations, one thought burned in his mind: whatever the truth about Arthur's betrayal, whatever game Novak was playing, this mission would end tonight - one way or another.

Chapter 16: Revelation

Five hours before game time, Andrei sat in his office at the ice rink reviewing final play strategies when the phone rang. The USSR Hockey Federation official's voice crackled through the line, announcing the semifinal's postponement due to "technical issues" with the cooling system.

Andrei made the appropriate noises of disappointment, his voice carrying just the right note of frustrated coach, but his mind raced. Technical issues. The phrase triggered a memory - fragments of conversation overheard during his captivity about the cooling system's crucial role in maintaining temperatures for the weapon test.

The pieces clicked into place. The KGB wasn't postponing the game for technical problems - they needed time to prepare the facility for the weapons test. The semifinal game would provide perfect cover, the crowd's attention focused on hockey while secret work continued in the restricted areas below.

Andrei's fingers drummed against his desk as he processed the implications. His gaze drifted to the window overlooking the ice, where workers were already setting up what appeared to be routine maintenance equipment. But he knew better - those weren't ordinary technicians down there.

His thoughts snapped back to the Yankees logo etched in the museum's basement window. At the time, it had seemed like a message about the missing agents' presence. But now, staring at the city map spread across his desk, Andrei saw something else. The museum's location - its proximity to the rink, its basement level, its age-worn architecture perfect for concealing secret chambers.

Within the hour, Andrei found himself back at the Vyatka Paleontological Museum, ostensibly examining the exhibits while his trained eyes cataloged every detail. The building's layout was typical of pre-revolution merchant mansions - a central hall with wings extending outward, and most importantly, an extensive basement system for storage and winter provisions.

He moved casually through the public areas, noting the thickness of the walls, the placement of support columns. If he were hiding prisoners with specialized technical knowledge, this would be the perfect location. Close enough to the ice rink for easy transport, but separate enough to maintain deniability.

A coded message from Arthur arrived that evening through their established church-flower seller-warehouse worker chain. Andrei's blood ran cold as he decoded the text:

"Extraction team compromised. Proceed solo. Priority remains: prevent test, secure agents. God speed."

The implications hit him like a physical blow. No backup. No extraction team. Just him, trying to simultaneously rescue the agents and stop a weapons test that could shift the balance of power in the Cold War.

The weight of his mission pressed down on him as he burned the message, watching the paper curl and blacken in his ashtray. Every aspect had become exponentially more difficult. Moving multiple hostages without support. Preventing a weapons test without backup. Ensuring everyone's escape with no extraction team.

Yet as he stared at the ashes of Arthur's message, a plan began to form. The very complexity of his situation might work to his advantage. The KGB would be looking for a team, for coordination, for standard extraction protocols. A single man moving quickly, decisively, might slip through their nets.

Andrei pulled out his notebook, sketching a rough layout of the museum's basement. The Yankees logo had been scratched at ground level, suggesting the agents were being held in outer chambers rather than the deeper storage areas. If he could get to them, move them quickly...

But first, he needed to confirm their location. One wrong move now would alert the KGB, and any change to their weapons test plans could prove catastrophic. He needed to be certain.

The clock on his wall ticked steadily, marking the passage of precious time. Five hours ago, he'd been a hockey coach preparing for a semifinal. Now he was planning a solo rescue operation while trying to prevent a secret weapons test. The absurdity of it almost made him laugh.

Almost.

Instead, Andrei bent over his notes, plotting trajectories and timing, marking possible entry points and escape routes. The game had changed, but the stakes remained the same - perhaps even higher. Without an extraction team, the margin for error had shrunk to nothing.

As night settled over Kirov, Andrei made his final preparations. He would move on the museum tomorrow, using his status as coach to establish an alibi while he reconnoitered the basement. Every step would have to be perfect, every moment precisely calculated.

The KGB thought they were being clever, using the postponed hockey game as cover. But they'd given Andrei exactly what he needed - time to act while they focused on maintaining their deception. Now he just had to make every second count.

The next morning, Vyatka Paleontological Museum had just opened its doors when Andrei strode in, carrying a stack of papers and wearing his most officious expression. Two KGB guards stood near the entrance, their eyes tracking his movement with predatory focus.

"Comrade Novikov," one of them stepped forward. "The museum is preparing for a private exhibition. I'm afraid-"

"Exactly why I'm here," Andrei cut in sharply, pulling out a document with the hockey federation's letterhead. "The team is scheduled for a cultural enrichment tour. Part of their training regime. Surely you received the notification?"

The guards exchanged uncertain glances. Andrei pressed his advantage, flipping through his papers with growing impatience.

"This is approved by the Ministry of Sport. The players will be here in twenty minutes. I need to verify the route, ensure it's appropriate for athletic personnel." He fixed them with his sternest coaching glare. "Unless you'd prefer to explain to the Ministry why our athletes were unprepared for the upcoming cultural questions in their evaluations?"

The mention of Ministry oversight worked its magic. The first guard stepped aside, though his eyes remained suspicious. "Of course, Comrade Coach. But the basement level is off-limits for... renovation."

"Naturally," Andrei nodded, already moving past them. "I'll need to see maintenance access points as well. Can't have our athletes trapped if there's an emergency, can we? Safety protocols, you understand."

His confident stride and bureaucratic reasoning carried him through the main hall. Andrei made a show of examining display cases and making notes, always moving with purpose. When he reached the basement door, he pulled out a maintenance checklist, studying it with exaggerated concern.

"This won't do at all," he muttered, just loud enough to be heard. "The emergency exits must be clearly marked. Ministry regulations are very specific..."

The door closed behind him, and Andrei descended into the shadows of the basement. His heart pounded, but his face betrayed nothing. Sometimes the best way to hide was in plain sight, using the very system they'd created against them.

The museum's basement air hung thick with dust and decay as Andrei moved silently through the shadows, counting doorways. The Yankees logo had been right - at the end of the main corridor, a heavy door stood slightly ajar, voices drifting from within.

Andrei's breath caught. American voices.

He eased closer, straining to hear the conversation. Voices drifted through the air, fragmented and indistinct—two men, discussing equations and trajectory calculations. He couldn't pinpoint where the sound was coming from, as if it was echoing from all directions at once. Before he could move, a sharp voice behind him froze him in place.

"We wondered when you'd find us."

Andrei turned slowly. A gaunt man in tattered clothes stood watching him, eyes sharp despite his haggard appearance. Another figure emerged from the shadows - the second agent.

"You're the American," the first man said quietly. "We hoped someone would notice our sign."

Andrei stepped forward, ready to outline his extraction plan, but the scientist raised his hand.

"We're not leaving," he stated flatly. "Not yet."

"What? You don't understand, I'm here to-"

"We understand perfectly." The second scientist moved closer. "They've got what they wanted from us. The guidance system is nearly complete. If we disappear now, they'll know something's wrong. They'll change everything - the test site, the timing, all of it."

The first scientist nodded. "Listen carefully. They're developing an ICBM with a revolutionary guidance system. Undetectable by current radar technology. The test is scheduled for the night of the semifinal game."

"The delivery system," Andrei pressed, keeping his voice low. "Tell me about it."

The scientist glanced nervously at the door, his hands trembling slightly. "That's the brilliant part - and the terrible part. They've modified the ice rink's cooling system to maintain critical temperatures for the guidance components. The entire facility is one giant temperature control unit, hidden in plain sight."

Andrei's mind raced, processing the implications. "So if we disrupt the cooling system..."

"The entire test fails." A grim smile crossed the scientist's face. "But it has to happen at exactly the right moment. Too soon, and they'll have time to adapt. Too late..."

The sound of footsteps in the corridor cut their conversation short. The scientists melted back into the shadows, leaving Andrei with a final whispered warning: "Stop the test. Then come back for us."

Later that night, Andrei met Taisiya in the back room of her bakery. Her face paled as he outlined what he'd learned.

"Sugar in the generators?" she whispered. "Flour in the weapons lab? It's suicide."

"It's our only chance." Andrei spread out a rough diagram of the ice rink. "You can arrange the deliveries without suspicion. Large bags of flour, sugar - normal bakery supplies."

Taisiya's hands trembled slightly as she studied the diagram. "And if something goes wrong? If they catch you?"

"Then you take these." Andrei slid a packet across the table - documents, maps, contact information. "Get yourself out. There's a car waiting in Leningrad. People who will help you cross the border."

Their eyes met in the dim light. Unspoken words hung between them, heavy with possibility and regret.

"I won't leave you," Taisiya said finally, her voice firm. "We do this together, or not at all."

Over the next hours, they refined every detail of their plan. Taisiya would arrange the deliveries, using her regular suppliers to avoid suspicion. The flour and sugar would arrive mixed with legitimate supplies, nothing to draw attention.

Andrei memorized the rink's maintenance schedule, identifying the perfect window to sabotage the generators. The flour placement would be trickier - too much in one spot would be noticed, too little would be ineffective. It had to be perfect.

They arranged multiple escape routes, each with its own set of documents and cover stories. Transportation was coordinated through Taisiya's network of trusted contacts - people who had their own reasons to help strike back at the regime.

As dawn approached, Andrei rolled up the last of their plans. Everything was in place. The next twenty-four hours would determine not just their fate, but potentially the course of the Cold War itself.

"Ready?" he asked softly.

Taisiya straightened her shoulders, her eyes hard with determination. "Ready."

Together, they stepped out into the gray Kirov morning, each carrying their portion of a plan that would either save them all or doom them to failure. The game was about to begin.

The first delivery arrived at the ice rink exactly on schedule. Taisiya supervised the unloading, her voice carrying across the loading dock as she berated the workers for their rough handling of her supplies.

"Careful with those! You think flour grows on trees?" She pointed to specific spots near the maintenance access. "Stack them there. No, there! These need to go to the kitchens later."

Through the loading dock windows, Andrei watched the performance while reviewing maintenance schedules. His practiced eye noted the guard rotations, the cameras' blind spots, the precise moments when security's attention wavered.

That night, after the last practice session, Andrei stayed late in his office. The cleaning crews had already finished - no one questioned a dedicated coach reviewing game films. He waited until the guard patrol passed his door for the third time, their footsteps echoing down the corridor at exactly twenty-three minutes past midnight.

Moving silently, Andrei slipped into the maintenance area. The generator room's lock yielded easily to the key he'd procured earlier. Inside, were the massive diesel generators that provided backup power for the rink and weapon's lab.

Working quickly, Andrei located the fuel storage tanks. The sugar, finely ground and mixed with diesel fuel in precise amounts, would crystallize in the engines at exactly the right moment - not too soon to raise suspicion, not too late to prevent the test.

A noise in the corridor froze him mid-pour. Footsteps approached, then passed. Andrei released his breath, finished the sabotage, and carefully removed all traces of his work. The generators lie waiting unaware of the destruction now lurking in their fuel lines.

The weapons lab proved more challenging. Security was tighter, but Andrei's coaching credentials gave him access to the adjoining ice rink areas. Over three careful trips, disguised as equipment checks, he distributed the flour. A fine dusting here, a sprinkle there, all in areas where routine cleaning wouldn't reach.

The flour's placement was critical. Too much powder would be visible, too little wouldn't achieve the necessary chain reaction. Andrei measured each deposit carefully, using ventilation patterns and structural blueprints memorized from his earlier reconnaissance.

Just before dawn on the morning of the test, Andrei met his small team in the bakery's back room one final time. The warehouse worker confirmed the escape vehicle's location. The night watchman reported on updated security patterns. Taisiya laid out the last of their forged documents.

"The timing has to be perfect," Andrei stressed, his finger tracing their escape route on a worn map. "Once the generators fail, we'll have minutes to be sure the rink is empty. Then flour ignition will be in stages. By the time they realize it's sabotage, it will be too late."

"And the scientists?" Taisiya asked, her voice tight with tension.

"They know to be ready. When the chaos starts, we move fast." Andrei met each person's eyes in turn. "If anything goes wrong, if we get separated, stick to your assigned routes. No one waits for anyone else."

The room fell silent as the weight of their mission settled over them. Weeks of planning, countless risks taken, all coming down to the next few hours. One mistake, one moment of bad timing, and they'd all face the consequences.

"Whatever happens," Taisiya said softly, breaking the silence, "we've chosen our path."

Andrei nodded, unable to voice the emotions tightening his throat. These people had risked everything to help him, driven by their own desires for freedom, their own hatred of the regime. Whatever their fates, they'd chosen to act rather than remain silent.

As his team filed out into the pre-dawn darkness, each taking separate routes to avoid suspicion, Andrei remained behind with Taisiya. There were no guarantees they'd all survive the next twenty-four hours. No certainty they'd succeed. But the pieces were in place, the trap was set.

Soon, the KGB would discover exactly how dangerous a cornered American agent could be. And if they were very, very lucky, they'd live to talk about it.

Andrei checked his watch one final time. In twelve hours, the game would begin - but not the one the Soviets were expecting.

Chapter 17:
The Final Game

The sharp smell of floor wax and stale sweat filled Andrei's small office as he made final adjustments to the team roster. On the surface, the lineup sheet looked like standard coaching strategy. But hidden within the player numbers and line combinations lay the coordinates and crucial details about the weapons test that had to reach Arthur.

Through his office window, Andrei watched KGB agents take their positions around the arena. They moved with practiced casualness, but their military bearing gave them away - too stiff, too alert for ordinary hockey fans. Novak would be watching too, though Andrei hadn't spotted him yet.

The crowd's rumble grew as game time approached. Andrei studied his notes one last time, committing the code patterns to memory before destroying the paper. Player 27 for longitude, 14 for latitude. Defensive pairings to indicate missile trajectory. Line changes would spell out the message one digit at a time.

"Coach?" A player appeared in the doorway. "Team's ready."

Andrei nodded, tucking his clipboard under his arm. Game time.

The first period started normally enough. Andrei waited until ten minutes in before making his first coded substitution, sending out an unusual combination of players - 27, 14, 32. Location coordinates, first sequence.

His assistant coach frowned at the lineup card. "Those wings haven't played together all season."

"Testing something," Andrei replied curtly, eyes fixed on the ice where the numbers were now clearly visible to any observer - including, he hoped, Arthur's man in the crowd.

The players struggled to find their rhythm with the unfamiliar combinations. Passes went astray, defensive coverage broke down. The opposing team scored twice in quick succession.

Murmurs of discontent rippled through the crowd. Andrei ignored them, focusing on his next sequence of numbers. Another line change, another piece of the message transmitted through seemingly random player combinations.

By the second period, his assistant was openly questioning the strategy. The players shot confused glances at the bench, trying to make sense of their coach's erratic decisions. But they were professionals - they played on, adapting as best they could to the constant shifts in personnel.

The KGB observers had noticed too. Andrei could see them conferring in the stands, their attention increasingly focused on the unusual pattern of substitutions. But they couldn't stop the game without causing a scene. Not with the packed arena watching every move.

The score remained close - too close. Andrei needed the game to continue, needed time to complete his transmission. Each goal against his team brought the risk of early substitutions, disrupting his carefully planned number sequences.

Tension mounted as the third period began. The crowd was fully invested now, living and dying with each shift in momentum. Even the KGB agents had gotten caught up in the game's flow, their surveillance wavering as the action intensified.

With five minutes remaining and the score tied, Andrei sent out his final combination. The coordinates were transmitted - now he just needed cover for what would come next. His team needed to win, but not too quickly. The timing had to be perfect.

The players, despite their confusion, had found a strange rhythm in the chaos. They compensated for unfamiliar linemates, covered for each other's mistakes. And with just thirty seconds left on the clock, something clicked.

A perfect pass from number 27 to 14 - the very numbers that had started his transmission. The puck hit the back of the net as the arena erupted. Players poured off the bench, crashing together in celebration. The crowd rose as one, their roar drowning out everything else.

In the midst of the chaos, Andrei moved with deliberate calm toward the maintenance corridor. The celebration provided perfect cover - no one noticed the coach leaving the bench, not with victory finally secured.

The crowd's cheers echoed through the arena's concrete halls as Andrei quickened his pace. The real game was about to begin, and he couldn't afford to waste the precious minutes of chaos the victory had bought him.

The victory celebration echoed through the arena as Andrei reached the maintenance corridor. In one swift motion, he yanked down the fire alarm. The piercing shriek cut through the crowd's cheers, replacing celebration with confusion, then panic.

"Fire! Everyone out!" The cry spread through the arena. The crowd surged toward the exits, order dissolving into chaos. KGB agents abandoned their posts, forced to assist with evacuation protocols. Even Novak, whom Andrei glimpsed directing his men, was fully occupied managing the stampeding spectators.

Andrei moved against the flow of the crowd, using the panic as cover to reach the electrical control room. His copied key worked smoothly in the lock. Inside, he located the main breaker and waited, counting down the seconds. The sugar he'd introduced into the generator's fuel system would need precise timing.

Three. Two. One.

The master switch clicked down. Darkness engulfed the arena. Emergency lights flickered, then failed as the contaminated backup generators sputtered and died. In the weapons lab below, crucial cooling systems began to fail.

Andrei navigated the darkness from memory, counting steps to the hidden entrance of the weapons lab. The security systems, disabled by the power failure, offered no resistance. Inside, the acrid smell of electrical burning mixed with the sweet scent of machine oil.

His fingers found the first flour deposit, carefully hidden in the ventilation system. Andrei pulled out a cigarette, his hands steady as he lit it. The ember glowed in the darkness as he calculated the burn rate. Seven minutes until the flame reached the flour.

He moved quickly through the lab, positioning two more cigarettes near strategic flour deposits. Each placement had to be precise - too close together, the reactions would be contained; too far apart, they'd fail to create the necessary chain reaction.

The final cigarette went near the largest flour cache, hidden in the ceiling tiles above the missile guidance system. Andrei checked his watch. Four minutes until the first cigarette ignited the flour. Time to move.

He was halfway up the stairs when the first explosion rocked the building. The flour-air mixture detonated with devastating force, the blast wave amplified by the confined space. Secondary explosions followed as the chain reaction spread through the lab.

The missile facility's reinforced walls, designed to contain the force of rocket testing, now trapped the explosive power of the flour detonation. Concrete cracked. Steel beams twisted. The entire structure shuddered as explosion after explosion tore through the complex.

Andrei emerged from the chaos. The blast had shattered windows throughout the arena. Smoke poured from the building as secondary fires spread. Emergency vehicles wailed in the distance, their sirens mixing with the screams and shouts of panicked citizens.

In the confusion, no one noticed one more figure slipping away from the destruction. Andrei moved quickly through the darkened streets, leaving behind a facility in ruins and a weapons test that would never happen. Now he just had to reach the museum before the KGB realized the explosion was no accident.

The city had been plunged into darkness and chaos. It was time for phase two - the rescue. And somewhere in the confusion, Taisiya would be waiting, ready to help him complete his mission. The real escape was about to begin.

The museum stood dark and silent as Andrei approached through the chaos-filled streets. Emergency vehicles screamed past, all attention focused on the devastated ice rink. The two KGB guards usually stationed at the entrance had disappeared, likely called to help contain the growing crisis.

Taisiya emerged from the shadows; two sets of maintenance uniforms draped over her arm. "Service entrance is clear," she whispered. "Your diversion worked perfectly."

They moved swiftly through the museum's empty halls, their footsteps masked by the distant sirens. The basement door yielded to Taisiya's stolen key. In the darkness below, Andrei clicked his flashlight twice - the predetermined signal.

"About time," a voice responded from the shadows. The two American scientists stepped into the beam of light, looking even more haggard than during Andrei's previous visit. "Quite a show you put on up there."

"Less talking, more moving," Andrei handed them the uniforms. "We have exactly eight minutes before the emergency response patterns shift."

Dressed as maintenance workers, they emerged into a city gripped by panic. The sky glowed orange from the ice rink fire, smoke casting an apocalyptic pall over Kirov. Perfect conditions for four people to disappear.

They split up according to plan - Andrei with one scientist, Taisiya with the other. Different routes, different checkpoints, all leading to the same destination. The city's emergency protocols actually worked in their favor, the confusion providing cover as they navigated the darkened streets.

Two hours later, in an abandoned hunting cabin, roughly fifty kilometers outside the city, the team reunited. The warehouse worker and night watchman had done their jobs perfectly - fresh clothes, documents, and a car with diplomatic plates waited for them.

As they changed into Western clothing, Andrei finally allowed himself to relax slightly. They'd done it. The weapons test was destroyed, the scientists rescued, and their escape route secure.

"I have to ask," one of the scientists said, pulling on a new shirt. "The flour explosion - that was inspired. Military demolitions training?"

"Baker, actually," Andrei smiled, nodding toward Taisiya. "I told her a story back in Buffalo where a flour mill exploded in the early 1900's"

"And the sugar in the generators?" the other scientist asked. "Brilliant way to ensure the cooling systems failed."

Taisiya laughed softly. "We had to make sure the flour had time to spread through the air before ignition. Sugar bought us the time we needed."

The first scientist shook his head in admiration. "All that, just from seeing our sign in the museum window."

"Speaking of which," Andrei turned to them, a glint of amusement in his eyes despite their still-dangerous situation. "Which one of you guys is the Yankees fan?"

The second scientist raised his hand, grinning despite his exhaustion. "Grew up in the Bronx. Couldn't resist leaving a message when I figured out another American was in town. Risky, but I had a feeling you'd understand."

"That logo saved your lives," Taisiya said softly. "And maybe a lot more, considering what they had you working on."

Silence fell over the cabin as they contemplated how close the Soviets had come to developing their undetectable missile. Outside, the first light of dawn was breaking over the Russian forest. Soon they would begin the next phase of their journey to freedom.

But for now, in this moment of relative safety, they allowed themselves to savor their success. Four people from different worlds, brought together by chance and courage, had managed to strike a blow against an empire.

Tomorrow would bring new dangers, new challenges. But they had overcome impossible odds once. They would do it again.

Chapter 18:
Return

The Buffalo Central Terminal bustled with its usual morning activity as John Kobczyk stepped off the train, Taisiya close by his side. The familiar sights and sounds of home washed over him, but his attention immediately fixed on the figure waiting near the platform's edge. Arthur, looking exactly as he had three months ago, stood with his hands in his pockets, an unreadable expression on his face.

"Welcome home, John," Arthur said, stepping forward. His eyes moved to Taisiya. "And this must be-"

"We need to get going," John cut in, shifting his bag to create a barrier between them. "Elana's waiting."

A flash of something - hurt? understanding? - crossed Arthur's face, but he simply nodded. "Of course. The car's outside."

The drive to John's house passed in tense silence. John could feel Taisiya's questioning glance, but he kept his eyes fixed on the passing streets of Buffalo. The questions burning in his mind about Novak, about Arthur's role in everything, would have to wait.

Elana stood on the front porch as they pulled up, her face breaking into a tearful smile at the sight of her brother. She rushed down the steps as John emerged from the car, pulling him into a fierce embrace.

"I prayed for you every day, I missed you so," she whispered, her voice thick with emotion.

"I'm home now," John replied softly, then turned to gesture Taisiya forward. "Elana, this is Taisiya."

The two women regarded each other for a moment before Elana's face softened. Without hesitation, she pulled Taisiya into a warm hug. "Welcome to America, dear. Welcome to our family."

John watched as his sister led Taisiya inside, already chattering about getting her settled and comfortable. The easy acceptance, the immediate inclusion of Taisiya into his family's circle, made his chest tight with emotion.

Arthur cleared his throat behind him. "John, we should talk."

"Yes," John turned, his voice hardening. "We should. Your office, one hour."

The familiar confines of Arthur's office felt different now as John entered an hour later. The place where he'd received so many mission briefings, shared so many victories and failures with his mentor, now seemed charged with unspoken accusations.

At the reception desk outside Arthur's door, a warm smile greeted him.

"Welcome back, John," Shirley's eyes sparkled with genuine affection. "It's so nice to have you back safe and sound."

"It's nice to be back," John replied, then leaned against her desk conspiratorially. "But you know what I need?"

"What is it, John?"

"One of those apple pies you bake for me. I just can't seem to make them like you can."

Shirley's eyes twinkled as she straightened some papers on her desk. "Well, we all must keep our secrets, John," she said with a knowing wink. "Go ahead, Arthur is waiting for you."

"Novak," John said without preamble, remaining standing. "Explain."

Arthur sighed, looking suddenly older. "Sit down, John. Please."

John remained on his feet. "You fed him information about my mission. About my communications with you. Why?"

"To save your life." Arthur's voice was quiet but firm. "We had intelligence suggesting Orlov was closing in. If he'd caught you at the ice rink during the actual operation, you wouldn't have made it out alive." Arthur sat intently while lighting his pipe.

"So you had me captured beforehand? By a KGB officer?"

"By a CIA asset who's been embedded in the KGB for years." Arthur leaned forward. "Novak's been our man from the start, John. His entire KGB career was crafted by us."

John's mind raced, reassessing every interaction with Novak in this new light. The careful interrogations, the conveniently malfunctioning equipment, the subtle warnings...

"The technical difficulties during questioning," John said slowly. "The way he kept providing me with cover stories..."

"All designed to establish your innocence while maintaining his cover." Arthur pulled out a file, spreading photographs across his desk. "Orlov was ready to move on you. He had a team in place at the ice rink. If you'd tried to execute your original plan..."

"I would have walked right into a trap." John finally sank into a chair, the full weight of what Arthur had done hitting him. "But why not just tell me about Novak?"

"Because you needed to react naturally to capture. Any hint that you were expecting it would have tipped our hand." Arthur's voice softened. "I couldn't risk losing you, John. Not just as an operative, but as... well."

The unspoken words hung in the air between them. John stared at his mentor, seeing past the spymaster to the man who had guided him, protected him, worried about him like a father.

"You should have trusted me with the truth," John said, but the anger had drained from his voice.

"Would you have trusted me with Taisiya's involvement?" Arthur countered gently.

John conceded the point with a slight smile. He stood, extending his hand across the desk. "Thank you. For watching out for me."

Arthur looked at the offered hand and shook his head. "Come here, you fool," he said gruffly, pulling John into a fierce hug. "Welcome home, son."

As they separated, both men quickly composed themselves, falling back into their familiar professional demeanor. But something had shifted, a deeper understanding reached between mentor and protégé.

John tossed a classified folder onto Arthur's desk. The bold letters on the cover read: "OPERATION: CRIMSON DECEIT." Arthur looked at it for a moment, then up at John, his eyes filled with unspoken questions.

John grabbed a pen from Arthur's holder and, with a swift motion, crossed out the mission title. In large, bold letters, he wrote: "OPERATION: HAT-TRICK."

Arthur raised an eyebrow. "What does that mean?"

John leaned back, a grin tugging at the corner of his lips. "It means I destroyed the weapons lab, I rescued the agents, and I've found a wonderful woman. That's three goals in one dangerous game."

Arthur blinked, momentarily taken aback, then let out a soft chuckle, shaking his head. "You really are something else, John."

"So," Arthur said, clearing his throat. "Tell me about this flour explosion idea. That was rather brilliant."

John smiled, settling back into his chair. The tension that had filled him since the train station finally eased. He was home, truly home, and the shadows of doubt that had clouded his relationship with Arthur had finally lifted.

The aroma of Elana's cooking filled the house as John and Arthur arrived for dinner. In the kitchen, Taisiya and Elana worked side by side, their laughter drifting through the doorway. Two worlds, once separated by an iron curtain, now merged over something as simple as preparing a meal.

"You should have seen her face when I showed her the electric mixer," Elana called out as they entered. "In ten minutes, she was teaching me three new ways to knead dough."

Taisiya smiled, her initial shyness giving way to comfort in this warm family setting. "In Kirov, we did everything by hand. But this..." she gestured at the modern appliances, "this is like magic."

The dinner table groaned under a mix of American and Russian dishes - Elana's pot roast beside Taisiya's piroshki, mashed potatoes sharing space with borscht. As they ate, stories flowed freely, carefully edited versions of their adventures bringing both laughter and shocked gasps from Elana.

"So there I was," John found himself saying, "trying to explain hockey strategies to a KGB agent while your piroshki sat in my pocket like a hot coal."

"Better than the time you had to hide those documents in the flour sack," Taisiya countered, her eyes twinkling. "Your hands were white for days."

Arthur raised his glass. "To new beginnings," he said simply. "And to family - both old and new."

Later that night, after the others had gone, John and Taisiya stood on the back porch of what would now be their home. The Buffalo night was cool but peaceful, so different from the tension-filled evenings in Kirov.

"Arthur offered me another assignment," John said quietly, watching Taisiya's reaction. "In Berlin."

Taisiya nodded slowly. "And?"

"I turned it down." He turned to face her. "I think there are enough battles to fight right here. The bakery needs renovating, for one thing."

"The bakery?" Taisiya's eyes widened.

"Well, we can't let all that talent go to waste, can we? Besides," he smiled, "I hear there's good money in wedding cakes."

Taisiya laughed, the sound carrying across the quiet yard. "From spy to baker. What would Novak say?"

"Probably that the best moves aren't always the obvious ones." John pulled her close. "What do you think? Ready to build something that doesn't involve international intrigue?"

"I think," Taisiya said softly, "that after all the destruction we've seen, creating something would be a nice change."

The next morning found them at the empty storefront that would become their bakery. Sunlight streamed through dusty windows, illuminating peeling paint and worn floorboards. But where others might have seen decay, they saw possibility.

John ran his hand along an old counter. "The oven will go there. Display cases along that wall."

"And here," Taisiya pointed to a corner, "a small café. Like the one where you first spoke to me."

They moved through the space, planning and dreaming. No code words needed now, no hidden meanings in their conversation. Just a man and a woman, building a future from the ashes of their past.

As they stepped back onto the street, the morning sun warming their faces, John felt a deep sense of peace settle over him. The game of shadows and secrets was over. A new chapter was beginning.

The baker and the spy, he thought with amusement. Not exactly a traditional love story. But then again, nothing about their journey had been traditional.

And as they walked hand in hand through the streets of Buffalo, John Kobczyk knew he wouldn't have it any other way.

Chapter 19:
Echoes

Six months after opening, the bakery had transformed from a quiet corner shop into a bustling hub, thanks to Taisiya's natural aptitude and John's discreet but steady support. With each week, their reputation spread across Buffalo's Polish district and beyond. Local residents lingered in the warm glow of the bakery on snowy mornings, leaving with hands full of sugar-dusted pryaniki and dark, spiced loaves. Inside, the air held a comforting warmth, heavy with vanilla and the faint scent of smoke from the woodstove—a quiet but constant reminder of the hard lessons both John and Taisiya had learned.

Taisiya, now wearing the American nameplate "Tasha" on her uniform, was the heart of the operation. She moved with an ease that belied her Russian roots, her English no longer hesitant but self-assured. Yet, John saw the way her hand trembled at times, a flicker of the past, before she regained her composure and smiled for a customer. Her accent softened with every interaction, but her Old World charm was unmistakable, and it enchanted those who walked through the bakery's doors. Taisiya had a way of making each visitor feel like an old friend, despite occasional stumbles over unfamiliar American idioms or a laugh that came too loud in the otherwise hushed shop.

Elana, John's sister, had become a steadfast ally. Over the months, she had quietly bridged the gaps between Taisiya's Eastern European stoicism and the exuberant American customs that Taisiya found so perplexing. Together, they spent countless evenings in the kitchen, Elana patiently explaining American recipes and customs, Taisiya listening with a mix of intrigue and cautious acceptance. On quiet mornings before the bakery opened, the two women would sit at the table, Elana teaching her the nuances of American manners while Taisiya reciprocated with old Russian tales, each story rich with her homeland's harsh winters and resilient people.

The bakery, too, had adapted, finding a middle ground that blended the rich flavors of Taisiya's heritage with a distinctly American charm. Taisiya's lessons, now held twice weekly, had drawn a loyal following, and she enjoyed the sight of her students attempting to master Russian pastries, their hands dusted with flour, cheeks flushed from the heat of the oven. Her classes became as much about cultural exchange as they were about cooking. To some of the older Polish women in Buffalo, Taisiya's knotted braids and deliberate, practical movements recalled their mothers and grandmothers. To the younger ones, she was a mystery, a foreign woman who moved gracefully between two worlds, one foot in the past and another in an uncertain future.

Andrei, now as much John as he could be, had integrated himself into the bakery's everyday rhythm, though he still kept a watchful eye on the door. Some nights, they lingered together after closing, sharing quiet moments that felt strange in their simplicity, as though the safety of a peaceful life was something foreign and precarious. In those moments, he would catch her watching him, her face a study in quiet joy and sadness, as if haunted by the ghosts they had left behind in Kirov.

Their conversations rarely touched on the past. Instead, they spoke of practical matters—the bakery's success, the strange twists of American holidays, or the stubborn oven that refused to hold an even temperature. But in the stillness of the kitchen, when the lights dimmed and the soft hum of the radio filled the air, the weight of all they had survived lingered in the silence between them.

One late evening, after they had scrubbed the counters clean and swept the flour from the floor, John caught her hand as she passed, pulling her close for just a moment longer. The softness of her touch, once hardened by the vigilance of her former life, was now steady and assured, her fingers intertwining with his as naturally as though she had been born here. They shared a look—one that held years of secrets, fears, and the hard-won relief of survival. No words were needed. They both knew the cost of finding this fragile peace.

As they locked up and stepped into the chilly night, the streets silent and heavy with snow, Taisiya's gaze drifted down the street, her hand clenching John's as they walked, her steps deliberate. Behind her, the light in the bakery window glowed softly, a beacon of a life neither had expected to find but had fought, in their own way, to keep. Together, they walked through the darkened city streets, blending into the quiet rhythms of a world that, at last, felt like their own.

Arthur had extended the invitation casually, as if it were a mere afterthought. “Why don’t we catch the Buffalo Bisons game this Saturday?” he’d suggested, his voice measured and neutral, though John sensed the undertow. Arthur was the type to choose his words like a craftsman, each phrase honed for precision. John hadn’t been to a hockey game since he’d returned. He had stepped back from working with the Bisons team. The rink, the scent of ice and sweat, the crowd’s fervor—it all held memories layered in smoke and shadow.

As they entered the arena, John felt the familiar surge of adrenaline, the noise and motion closing in around him. The smell of wet concrete and the cold bite of the ice prickled his senses, grounding him in a way that was both comforting and unsettling. His gaze scanned the rink and the stands, cataloging the people milling around: couples laughing, kids leaning over the railings, men in caps clutching cups of beer. Arthur, with his wife, Martha, by his side, led the way to their seats, while John walked alongside Tasha. It should have felt harmless, yet he couldn’t shake the instinct that had kept him alive for years—that inclination to observe, to evaluate. As they reached their seats, John caught his own reflection in the plexiglass along the rink’s edge, and for a split second, the image blurred between the man he was now and the agent he had once been.

Taisiya, or Tasha as she was now known, settled beside him, her gaze alight with curiosity. She was still adjusting to the language, the customs, the unspoken codes of America. Yet, she seemed at ease here, chatting with Arthur and Martha about the Bisons and nodding with interest as Arthur pointed out the notable players on the roster. Watching her adapt so seamlessly to this world stirred something deep within him. It was a strange feeling to see her blend in so well while he sat there, the weight of old instincts making him feel like an outsider.

Their conversation was light, sprinkled with laughter, yet undercut with tension only John felt. Arthur leaned forward, smiling as he gestured at the players warming up, his eyes scanning the crowd with what seemed like casual disinterest. But John knew better. Arthur's body language was too careful, his voice a shade too neutral. This wasn't just a game; it was a test, another move on the board, and he was being watched as closely as he was watching.

The game began, and the crowd surged with a roar, all eyes glued to the ice as players clashed and skated in a ballet of speed and force. John leaned forward, his gaze trained not just on the puck but on the patterns, the coordination, the way each man's movements told a story. Old instincts rose unbidden, his mind tracking each pass, each body check, each player's stride. It wasn't about the game, not really; it was the focus, the awareness of every small detail that brought him back to a life he had tried to leave behind.

To his right, Taisiya laughed at some joke Arthur made, her voice carrying over the crowd's din. She seemed unaffected, unaware of the gravity that hung in the air. The clash of blades on ice, the sharp crack of a slapshot, the rise and fall of the crowd's cheers—it all sank into John like a familiar but unwelcome memory. He had been trained to notice patterns, to seek the gaps, to find the weak spots and exploit them. The muscle memory returned without permission, his mind slipping back into that dark rhythm where a misstep could cost lives.

Beside him, Arthur leaned in, his voice barely audible above the noise. "Hockey's a game of strategy, wouldn't you agree?" His tone was light, almost conversational, but the question hit a little too close.

John's gaze remained on the players, but his response was sharp. "Everyone has a role. A plan." His voice was barely above a whisper, but Arthur caught the edge in his tone.

The Zamboni rumbled across the ice between periods, its methodical patterns hypnotic. Martha touched Arthur's arm. "I'm going to grab some drinks. Taisiya, would you help me carry them?" The two women departed up the concrete steps, their heels clicking against each stair until they disappeared into the crowd near the concession stands. John watched them go, noting how the space around him and Arthur suddenly felt different - charged with possibility now that they were alone.

These moments were rare now, moments when the masks could slip, if only slightly.

Arthur leaned back, crossing his arms casually, but his gaze was intent. "Seems like you're settling in nicely," he said, his voice mild, though his eyes probed beneath the surface. "Quite a change from where you started."

John's jaw tightened, but he kept his face blank. "It's a simpler life here," he replied evenly, his gaze fixed on the empty ice. "No shadows lurking around every corner."

Arthur chuckled, though the sound held little humor. "Shadows have a way of finding people, no matter where they go. Especially people with... certain skills."

John remained silent, feeling the weight of Arthur's gaze. The game resumed, the players skating out with renewed energy, but neither man paid attention to the action on the ice.

Finally, John broke the silence, his tone cautious. "It's strange, isn't it? Being able to watch something so... normal. No risks, no agendas. Just a game."

Arthur's eyes flickered, his expression unreadable. "Not everyone sees it that way."

The loaded silence returned, and they both knew it was only a matter of time before the inevitable question surfaced. John's heart pounded as he chose his words carefully, aware that this exchange was a game in itself—a dance of truths and half-truths, where every response was a move on a chessboard.

After a moment, he turned to Arthur, his voice low but direct. "Do you think we'll ever really be done with it? With the Russians?"

Arthur's gaze was steady, his face impassive, though something flickered in his eyes—a flicker of the man he had once been, before duty and war had carved lines into his face. He didn't answer right away, and John felt the air around them grow heavy with unspoken truths.

Finally, Arthur exhaled, a long, measured breath. "The Cold War isn't a fight we'll ever walk away from, John. Not completely. We may think we can leave it behind, pretend it's someone else's problem, but it has a way of seeping into everything. Every game, every conversation, every decision."

John nodded, feeling the weight of Arthur's words settle over him like a mantle he couldn't shake. The crowd's cheers rose again as a goal was scored, but the sound felt distant, detached. The game continued on, but here, in the quiet space between them, was a reminder that they were still on a battlefield of sorts—one with no clear lines or endings.

"Art," John's voice was quiet, measured. "Do you ever ask yourself?"

Arthur glanced at him, eyebrows raised. "What's that, John?"

John's eyes swept the arena, making sure no one was within earshot. "Do you ever ask yourself if the Russians are pulling a stunt like I did, right under our noses?"

The words hung in the air between them. Arthur's face remained impassive, but something flickered in his eyes - a shadow of doubt, perhaps, or recognition. He said nothing, but his silence spoke volumes. The question lingered, unanswered, as the game played on below. Suddenly, Arthur's expression softened into a smile as he leaned forward. "Enough with the politics," he said, raising his beer. "A toast for a successful mission. John, you're back home safe - here's to you two and new beginnings."

The women's return brought a shift in the air, their laughter preceding them down the steps. Taisiya balanced three beers while Martha carried hot dogs wrapped in paper. They settled back into their seats, and John noticed how Taisiya's shoulders relaxed as she handed him his drink, unaware of the weight of the conversation she'd missed. She leaned close to tell Martha something about the game, her voice carrying that slight trace of accent that only emerged when she was excited. Arthur caught John's eye over their wives' heads, a silent understanding passing between them - some conversations were better left in the shadows where they belonged.

When the final whistle blew, the crowd erupted into cheers, and Taisiya clapped along, her face flushed with excitement. But as they left the rink, the conversation between John and Arthur hung in the air, a reminder of the lives they had led and the battles that remained. The world was shifting, moving into an uncertain future, but some things would never truly change.

And as John held Taisiya's hand, leading her through the throngs of fans spilling into the chilly Buffalo night, he felt the weight of his own unanswered questions, a shadow that would follow him long after the lights of the arena faded from view. The game might be over, but the war was far from done – They were all still playing, whether they chose to or not.

www.ingramcontent.com/pod-product-compliance
Lightning Source LLC
LaVergne TN
LVHW010548160826
845677LV00013B/3050
* 9 7 9 8 2 1 8 5 6 5 4 2 8 *